Tainted With Blood

By Brian Potter

STHENOTYPE

Cover art by Michael Allen
Editing by Stepheni Potter

First Edition 2025

ISBN 979-8-9923513-1-6

Published by SthenoType
Medford, NJ 08055
www.SthenoType.com

One page at a time, sweet angel.
One careful turn, into blank pages that fill with ink
as we read on to each other.

The ink must dry before we turn another.
The smudges of prior pages teach us patience.

- Brian Potter

Foreword

By: Michael Allen

When I started SthenoType there was only one name I had in mind for the first story I wanted - Brian Potter.
I met Brian in high school, he was on stage and I was running the spotlights for a school play. A couple years later we worked together in retail and would spend the hours talking about various roleplaying games, which I was completely oblivious to. He opened my eyes to collaborative storytelling and RPGs, which would become one of my favorite hobbies.

I remember trying to understand how the mechanics worked, and all the math and rules, and he was sure to tell me that the "rule of cool" overrode everything. If it was clever, fun, innovative and the Game Master (GM) allowed it, it was in. That lead to us talking about the GM role and I mentioned it was kind of sad that a person has to sit and tell the story while the players get to have fun. With a sparkle in his eyes he informed me that it was just the opposite. Yeah, it's fun to play, but the GM gets to create an entire world! Every time the party gets together, they get to create environments, buildings, mazes, puzzles, and characters. Listening to him talk about throw-away characters he'd create for an interaction with the players, and hearing the voices and passion he had for telling the story always stuck with me, even 20 years later as I hatched a plan to get him to write me a book.

I could fill pages of the stories he'd tell and what our friendship meant to me. I'm heartbroken to release this book posthumously, but I'm glad you got a chance to tell the world a story. Rest easy, my friend.

Preface

By: Stepheni Potter

My Husband, The Storyteller

You always had a way with words. Whether they were your words or borrowed from the wit of others, it was your charming delivery that always swept me off of my feet and took my breath away.

I'm so happy that you chose to write this story first. It's been an honor to be part of this story from the very beginning, long before Mike approached you with an offer to publish whatever you decided to put on paper. When it came time to proofread and edit the first book, I was more than a little protective of it because it's so dear to me. I guarded it more than a typical proud, supportive partner would as your debut novel came together. It wasn't just your story. It was ours.

I could tell your readers about your writing process, but we both know that it was unorthodox, to say the least, and it was more frustrating at times than you'd ever admit in an author's interview. Instead, I'm going to share my favorite moment in bringing this story to life. It's one I loved to tell you, and one I hope that age will never steal from my memory.

For your readers who aren't aware, this story began in the same place as most of our favorites: at the roleplaying table. Living with four other roommates at the time in the aptly named "Commune," we had a regular rotation of games that we'd play with our friends. One day, you finally garnered enough interest for a Hunter: The Reckoning™ game. As much as you loved fantasy and supernatural elements, you were always drawn to the "normies" of any given setting. You wanted to be a smuggler in Star Wars, a hunter in World of Darkness, you despised nearly all superheroes except for The Incredibles, and the role of bard in Dungeons & Dragons might as well have been written for you. You avoided using magic or mystical power whenever possible, always feeling the need to prove that every party needed an average guy with a quick wit and an ability to get through situations without a sword or a lightsaber. So the irony that you finally found a party to play your favorite setting, that should be made up of a bunch of regular Joes, and it ended up having a handful of supernatural characters was not lost on you. Thankfully that didn't stop you from running the game. You would much rather have played in it, but you knew this was as close as you'd get to a Hunter campaign among our group who preferred more powerful and magical settings.

Our party started as it normally does, with a tenuous trust in each other and each working towards their own goals. One by one, the other players either resolved their characters' conflicts or simply lost interest and wrote themselves out of the story. During that time, you and I had gotten married and found an apartment for just the two of us to start our own family. The "Commune" family went their separate ways but we had some unfinished business. The Hunter story wasn't done. It was down to just Alex and me as your players. You said there were only a few sessions worth of story left and we weren't willing to leave it up in the air.

For your readers, when I said I am protective of this story, it's because Melissa and Tanya were my characters. The story deviated a little between the table and the page, but you always asked my opinion to see if they were reacting as they should when you made changes. I obviously love both versions of the story, but everything I've described up to now is just the leadup to what I feel to be the most immersive, emotional storytelling session I've ever been part of. (Spoiler alert for the first book ahead.)

It was time for the club scene, where Melissa and Tanya both ended up at Leila's big party. Alex was there with his character, who was a large inspiration for Mo. We settled in with whatever our takeout dinner was that night and listened as you described the scene. I decided to settle into the mindset of the vampire sister and watched everything unfold before me as your words filled the room.

As the club lights went down, I felt a heavy stillness settle in.

A spotlight shone on Leila as she dangled from wires over the stage, and I felt my breath leave my lungs and refuse to reenter.

I saw the wires dig into her wrists and arms as they suspended her full body weight. I licked my lips as the blood dripped onto the stage.

The stage hands slowly lowered her as she hung, crucified and grinning. All I could hear was a pounding heartbeat. I couldn't tell if it was mine, or hers, or Alex's, or the thunder of every other human heart in the crowd.

Finally, Leila's feet touched the stage and the large bodyguards reached for the wires to release her. Suddenly the spotlight cut out for a second, maybe two, and when it came back on, she stood with the large man in her arms, feeding on him before the deathly silent crowd. My skin felt like it was on fire and I had yet to blink. I didn't dare look away from the image that was set before me. Had I breathed? I couldn't tell.

When the lights came back up on stage and the party resumed, I felt my breath return and my heart slowed to its normal pace. We continued on with the game but I knew I had experienced something just then.

Majesty.

Leila had the trait known in World of Darkness™ as Majesty, but I'd actually felt it... because you had it.

You had the ability to root me to the spot and completely enrapture me with just your voice and your words. It was only a few minutes but I rode that high for hours. Years later, whenever we'd reminisce about our favorite sessions, that was always the one I'd tell. You would always smile, proud of yourself but in quiet humility. Your eyes drank it all in, hardly believing that it had such an effect on me almost twenty years later. Every time I'd retell it, I could feel my heart start to pound again and the fiery itch returned to my skin. I feel like you could see it, the power of your words wash over me again.

When this story was put to the page in **Bought with Blood**, your words entranced me again as it took me on new twists and turns. Now you've taken it beyond anything we played at the table in **Tainted with Blood** and made it your own, with just a little help by borrowing another character of mine who never got his moment in the sun. Thank you for giving them all one more breath of life.

Thank you for breathing the love of the story into me.

Thank you for our stories. All of them.

I love you, my storyteller.

My author.

My everything.

Chapter One - Cold Open

Blake tossed his mop of sweaty hair out of his face and turned around just as the sturdy bar of a folded steel chair smashed between his eyes. He reeled backward and flipped over a rope to the ring's apron and then to the floor a few feet below.

He could hear what sounded like the small crowd's cheers echoing around him before a loud ringing filled his head and the bright lights above swarmed his blurred vision.

"It's over for now." He could hear Simon's voice cut through the noise as if he was underwater.

Blake rolled over as a rush of blood from his broken nose ran down his lips. He rose to his knees just as a plastic cup of warm beer hit him in the chest and splashed into his face. He threw his head back as if he had just taken another hard shot from his opponent.

The crowd sounds of whistles and cheers came back to him. He blinked hard several times to squeeze the salt and sweat out of his eyes.

The audience chanted the count along with a voice inside the ring that belonged to a staggering referee. "THREE! FOUR!"

Blake climbed to his feet and reached up for the ring ropes to help him up onto the apron where he rolled inside to stop

1

the count. The fans chanted the name of Blake's opponent, a young stud with a salon tan and statuesque physique.

"MURPHY! MURPHY! MURPHY!"

Blake stood in time to duck and run under another chair swing, rebounded off the ropes, and flung his body into a twist to deliver a spinning wheel kick to the upper body of his opponent.

Murphy was struck with his hands raised to soften the blow and both men's bodies hit the mat. Blake stood quickly and threw his hands out at his sides as he turned to face each section of the audience. He shouted at the crowd as they booed loudly with their fists in the air in response. He dropped to a knee and held his head in one hand. With the other hand, he reached over and took a handful of Murphy's platinum blond hair to pull him up to a sitting position.

Blake looked out at the crowd to posture with a grimace. He grabbed a second handful of blond hair to strike with an unguarded head butt that landed with a sickening smack between their skulls. He knelt over Murphy, who fell flat with his arms splayed, before covering his knocked-out opponent with an elbow pushed across Murphy's jaw.

As the referee slapped his count of three on the mat, Blake grunted with labored breath into the other wrestler's ear, "There's always something else."

The crowd booed and threw trash into the ring as the referee checked on the loser of the match. He crossed his arms into the air toward the entrance aisle and responding EMTs rushed to the ring with a gurney.

Blake slumped over out of the way and rolled out of the ring holding his head again as he lumbered back the aisle through the curtain.

An announcer called out to the crowd with an echoing microphone. "Your winner by pinfall, JERRY RIGGS!"

Another emergency response worker wearing gloves sat Blake down on a nearby stool backstage to check him over.

The medical technician got in close to see better and pushed Blake's hair out of his face. "That was a messy hit, pal. I'm gonna have to set this nose. Hold still."

Blake closed his eyes while chilled enswells were pressed on either side of his nose, and then cotton swabs were adjusted inside his nostrils. A moment later, strong thumbs pressed against the cartilage of his nose and firmly but slowly realigned his airways with pressure working downward from the bridge.

"Swelling should come down soon enough. Might want to get a cab tonight to be safe." The EMT gave Blake a heavy slap on the shoulder and then removed his gloves. "Little steam in the showers couldn't hurt either. Your head alright after that shot?"

"Yeah," Blake nodded. "Occupational hazard. Thanks, doc."

Blake stood and slowly made his way to the locker room. He sat and pulled up the leather pant legs to unlace his boots and roll off his socks when the promotion manager leaned against the door frame.

"Sloppy shit out there, Gentry," he said as his pendulous belly stretched a tucked button-down shirt. "Not only do you look like hell and you changed my booking, but they carted Murphy out. So here's what I'm gonna do." He took a few steps and pulled his sagging pants up into place. "You're suspended until Murphy is cleared to return. And when you come back, you're gonna put that kid over, you hear me?'

Blake unhooked the five-point black belt harness from his torso and let it hang down. He continued removing his wrist tape and joint pads as he argued. "Look, Stan, that kid is still too green. How many chances are you gonna give him before he kills somebody out there? He can't lift, he can't hold, he doesn't sell for shit. Hell, he was gassed out the whole match. And you want me to carry him through another fight?"

"You will if you want to get paid," Stan answered. "You got your receipt, hot-head. And he'll get the win and push I promised. You heard that crowd," Stan pointed toward the arena. "They want him, not this BDSM biker bit you're doing out there. But come back, put him over, and keep training the others on off-nights, and you'll still get the bonus in your contract."

Stan straightened his tie and left the locker room as Blake stripped to shower. He dragged his fingers across the shaved sides of his head and hung his long hair over his face in the steaming sprayer to wash out the sweat and blood.

"That went well," Blake muttered to the drain in the floor.

***

Simon rolled his forehead across a barkless section of a tree to cool his head. He let out a gout of steamed breath and turned to sit against the trunk. Despite the early January cold, he and the others had worked themselves to a soaked sweat to keep on the move.

Reno spat near his feet and rolled his neck as he paced close by. "We can't keep running. And now we're too exhausted to put up a fight." He wiped his face and head with both hands and flicked away the sweat in frustration. "And why are we back here again? We're too close to the river."

Simon kept his eyes closed and listened to the pack moving about. "We're close to the river because they might think we crossed and split themselves up. If we have to defend ourselves, any tricks to keep numbers in our favor can be useful," he replied the same as when Sam asked what his plan was hours ago.

The rushing river could be heard just down the hill. It had risen with the recent rains and stirred up the scents of loose soil and debris against its banks.

Reno stopped his pacing and strode to stand over Simon. "And I told you it's too damn cold to make any difference," he retorted. "Stop second-guessing me. I told you I'd find us a place to settle."

Simon stood and glared back. He couldn't help but notice that Reno's posture was aggressive and his fists balled.

"I'm just trying to help keep us alive," Simon said quietly. "New territories bring new problems. And my gut tells me there's something else here. Like it's drawing me back every time we get too far from it. We're not just running from a rival pack anymore. There's something out there trying to get to us. I can feel it deep down."

"I feel it, too," Mama offered as she stood beside both men, looking up at their faces nearly touching at the nose. "Like a fog in my lungs every time we slow down. Stalking me from within."

Reno turned and kicked a dead branch on the ground. "And what I feel is that we're running in circles. That we're listening to a delirious old man who betrays the beast every chance he gets instead of listening to it. That we're tired and hungry. But, hey! At least we're not lost, right?" He threw up his hands and turned away, looking at the vast woods around them. "That would be a terrible mistake!"

"You'd know best how to spot a mistake, wouldn't you?" Simon challenged.

Sam looked up suddenly from retying her boot and Reno shot a look back at her with his lips between his teeth.

"That's enough, boys," Mama shushed at them. "We're in this

together. All of us."

"All but Josh," Simon muttered.

Reno's flesh tore away and he grew to his full beastly potential. He snarled and lunged at Simon, who dove out of the way and let Reno crash into the tree behind him.

Mama's features snapped as well, into a lithe, charcoal-furred wolf that leaped onto Reno's back and sunk her teeth into the nape of his broad neck to hang on as Reno's beast bucked and clawed, trying to get to her.

Another wolf ran into the fray and jumped at Reno, latching onto a leg. Simon recognized Fisher's scent and stripe of brown fur as he shouted at Sam. "Get out of here! Get away from him!"

Simon, too, shaped himself into a smaller, four-legged form that would allow him to outrun the monstrous killing machine Reno had become. He howled loudly and ran to cross the river.

Chapter Two - Second Skin

Tanya turned the key to lock the door of the second-hand clothing store and noted in the glass a hooded, shadowy figure coming close behind her. She removed the key and placed it into her purse before she pulled a small handgun and spun around.

The figure held up both hands, holding a brown paper bag in one and a small bouquet in the other. He used the bouquet hand to pull down his hood.

Mo shook his head slowly, "One of these days, you're gonna hurt somebody with that thing."

Tanya grinned and leaned on one hip as she put the handgun back into her purse. "And one of these days, maybe you'll learn not to sneak up behind someone."

"T, I told you I was on my way with supper," Mo said.

The bottom of the bag ripped just as Tanya slowly blinked away Mo using her initial instead of her name, the way only her sister would. "And I told you I don't like it when you call me that." She looked down at the containers on the sidewalk. "I never order Chinese takeout in the city anymore. Their bags are cheap."

Mo bent to salvage the spill as Tanya approached to help. She picked up a split cup and liquid poured across the cement into a crack. Mo had to stifle himself from shouting. "Aw, great! So much for the boba. The rest looks okay though. At least I didn't drop the flowers, huh?"

"I'd have preferred the tea. It's been a long day," she answered coldly. "Why flowers, anyway?"

"Thought it might cheer you up. You said this time of year is pretty rough," Mo replied as he hoisted what was left of the food bag with both hands.

Tanya brushed a wave of hair behind her ear and took the flowers to carry. "I guess the holidays will always be like that when someone is missing. At least they're done for another year."

"I don't know what to say. It's been, what? Five years?"

"Six," she corrected.

"Right. Six. Don't you think it's time to focus on other things?" Mo asked with a hopeful look.

Tanya spun on him and he nearly dropped the ripped bag again. The streetlight above flicked out, as it often did, as she advanced as if in a dim strobe. "I think I've done an awful lot since that night, thank you very much! I run my own business. I don't jump when the phone rings anymore. On YOUR advice for closure, I reopened my wounds and told my parents that Missy's GONE! I only hear from them DURING the holidays now, thanks again. So now I guess I have to put on my big girl panties every day and remind

9

myself in one more way how alone I am in this damn city, huh?"

Mo put the food on the hood of his car and turned to console her but she had already slammed the door from the inside of her convertible and turned the key in the ignition.

The lights flicked but the engine didn't turn over. Tanya kicked the floorboard and punched the steering wheel before she tried again, but only heard a click as she began to cry. Her hot breath fogged the glass of her frosted windshield.

The minutes dragged by before she heard a car door beside her. Then another. Then Mo came and tapped on her window. "Hey, look, my bad. I was outta line. Let me drive you home. You can eat on the way if you want, and I'll come back and take the car to Blake's shop in the morning, okay?"

She waited a little longer. She refused to look up and acknowledge him standing out in the cold. Tanya pressed her sleeve into her cheeks and opened the door. Without speaking, she nodded and reached out to hug Mo. Her nose pressed into the top of his hooded sweater from the height difference. She looked up as the streetlight winked out again and saw the full moon barely peeking through heavy clouds.

"Come on, I got you," Mo assured her as he turned to open the passenger door of his car. He hustled around and climbed in behind the wheel. "You can adjust the heat or radio or whatever if you want. We better get going, it's starting to snow."

"Hey," Tanya started. Her mouth hung open a moment as she chose her words. "I'm… I could still use a drink. Not that you owe me one or anything. You got something at your place? My fridge is empty."

Mo pulled his hood down and nodded with a comforting smile. "Yeah, like I said. I got you."

***

"Right this way, Mr. Solomon," a woman's low, sultry voice guided from the dim, chilly, echoing corridor to a room with a heavy vault-like cellar door. The hostess, on her clicking high-heels, escorted the man inside to find it was already crowded with several others. She robotically asked him to confirm that he was the last guest expected to arrive before she thanked him and retreated to close the door with a heavy metallic clank.

Melissa was blindfolded and her tongue flicked involuntarily against her teeth in rhythm with the strongest, or perhaps just the nearest, heartbeat to her. Her wrists and ankles were bound with thin, almost cutting, leather straps that stretched her into a pose to mimic Da Vinci's Vitruvian Man. She was centered in the room, just a few feet away from the wall farthest from the door, to leave space for interaction.

Aside from her strict bonds, she was dressed only in shining black high-heeled shoes, tight black bikini panties, a satin blindfold, a costume wimple, and broad black tape aligned like crucifixes over her nipples. She held still as a mannequin, with clean, inhumanly pale skin.

11

The man who had just entered was walking around the room with quiet, gliding footsteps, stirring his recently reapplied cologne in with the bouquet of perfume and sweat and liquor and acrid cigar breath, when he began to speak.

"My friends, I apologize for my tardiness. I'll keep things brief so we may begin to enjoy our time here. I am told that our young subject here has quite a tolerance for pain, both physical and mental. As you might expect, I've looked into her background, to find that she came into this profession directly from serving a few years within a cloistered convent. I've yet to uncover which that was, but find it interesting nonetheless as our present company has yet to relinquish her vow of silence."

The man speaking stepped closer, with a sound made as if he were opening a heavy trunk. "We have come to test that vow, my friends. Who among you is so unashamed of their sin before our sweet sister here, that they would care to cast the first stone?"

She did not waver within her bound state. She remained still and listened as a chatter arose within the room. Pieces of furniture were moved with metallic scraping on the hard floor. Low muttering carried about and echoed with blended words of excitement.

A cord of leather split the air and wrapped around her waist with a heavy crack of its tail. When she did not move or flinch, another whipping came that wrapped over her shoulder and cracked around her throat. Again she remained still as the fervor of her audience mounted.

12

As each took their turn, Melissa was assaulted over and over again with a variety of implements. Some were meant to be toys for those aroused by pain play. Others were workshop tools or weapons. One man chose to use his bare knuckles until he tired himself while she hung, returning her face forward almost defiantly after each strike. Her skin was broken and cut on nearly every exposed part of her body without so much as a whimper. Her assailants would often wait with heavy breaths and awestruck gasps as her skin healed before they inflicted more damage.

When the guests had tired and agreed they were satisfied, the room broke into applause, though it was unclear if the celebration was for her or each other. Their clapping and cheering echoed in the closed space and eventually quieted to a pregnant silence.

Melissa could hear the quiet, gliding steps drawing near again, then a gust of thick cigar smoke touched her face in a cloud. When she did not choke or turn away, the spectators made hushed sounds of approval.

The same man's voice from before spoke again, close to her ear. "I think I shall have to have you for future parties for those who have missed out tonight. Think about your price for private services and have your Madame contact me just as soon as possible. The fact that you didn't utter even the slightest outcry has my curiosity desperately aroused in a way I cannot better describe at this time."

He walked around behind her, tugging on her restraints to release them at each of her wrists and ankles. "I do believe tonight's fun has concluded," he announced. "I wouldn't care to bear the guilt of anyone having an accident in this weather beginning outside." He punctuated his closing words by reaching around Melissa's neck and crushing the lit end of his cigar between her breasts.

Still, she did not move nor retaliate. She refused to even so much as grunt or curl a lip at his obvious attempt to get an unrestrained reaction. She waited patiently as the party rejoiced and gathered at the door to leave. Melissa remained in her place until the hostess had seen everyone out and came to remove her blindfold and pay her fee.

Chapter Three - A Gentleman Never Asks

The morning sun reflected brightly over the dusting of snow that fell overnight. Simon squinted and blew labored breaths and shivered as he raised his arms to untie his hair. His soaked, heavy locks hung over his face as he bent forward to rest with his hands on his knees. His head was searing hot and he welcomed the trickling sweat over his face in the cold wind.

He looked over his shoulder at the faraway tree line and saw shimmering darkness between the branches. If not for the winter weather, he could have excused the mesmerizing movements as a dense flock of starlings rather than the toothy veil that whispered to him in a language he could not comprehend.

Simon shook his head and rubbed his eyes. The dawn's reflection and shaking of his head did his tired eyes no favors. When the flash of lights faded from his blurred vision, the strange, dark veil between the trees had gone and the leafless branches went on as far as he could see.

The full moon still hung visibly in a clear sky. He gave it a nod of thanks and winced in pain again before turning to face the city limits. Simon knelt and dragged his fingers across the snow and packed a fistful to press against his forehead.

Looking again at the distance ahead to travel, then down at his state of dress in tattered pants and a ripped t-shirt, he

15

once again willed his form to four legs as a wolf and took a few licks of the refreshing dusted snow. His ears perked toward the woods again as the whispering veil returned and beckoned him toward it.

Simon turned away from the dark illusion and broke into a run toward the city.

***

Tanya woke to the sound of a woman's voice in another room quick-fire muttering in Spanish. She looked down at herself in relief to see she was still fully clothed, except for her shoes, in the black leggings and red flannel shirt she'd worn the night before. She sat up quietly and listened as she ran her fingernails through her blonde hair and fixed it into a messy bun with an elastic band from her wrist.

Mo's bedroom was in disarray and smelled of dust as though it was rarely used or cleaned. Stacks of magazines were piled in the corner near a closed, sliding closet door. The walls held some movie posters and collectible items like prop swords and framed comic books.

She began looking around for her strapped high heel shoes when the door opened suddenly. Mo's sister, Gianna, poked her head in with a disapproving look that turned immediately to surprise.

"Um, hey," Gia said as she stepped inside the room. "You're about the last person I thought I'd find in here."

Tanya stood up and shrugged awkwardly and fiddled with her hands. "Yeah, me too."

"Oh, come on, girl. You could do worse," Gia winked. She put a hand on her waist and looked around the cluttered room with a laugh. "Well, maybe."

Tanya shook her head and made room to pass Gia through the door, still looking around for her shoes. "Nothing happened. My car broke down and Mo just happened to be there, like always, and we had a couple of drinks to unwind."

Tanya pointed to a blanket balled up in the corner of the microsuede sofa in the living room. "See? He slept on the couch."

"Alright," Gia said with her hands up. "Not like it's any of my business. I'm just sayin' you really could do worse, you know?"

Tanya found her shoes and leaned against the back of the couch to pull them on as she looked around the room. "Well, he's had plenty of time to ask me if he was interested. Years, in fact. And he's always so busy, he-"

"Years he spent working hard and putting himself through school," Gia cut her off and pointed when she addressed Tanya. "Years spent helping you put out flyers and set up and run a website for your new business. Years he spent saving up for a place of his own and a decent, reliable car. Years he spent helping me out when I got evicted, and he worked two jobs THAT whole year to pay my rent AND his so we wouldn't have to live together."

Gia went to the kitchenette and slammed a chair into its place under a small table. She screwed the cap back onto an almost empty bottle of liquor and took the empty glasses next to it to rinse in the sink.

Tanya stood with her arms crossed, looking at the floor, and took a breath to speak.

Gia put up a finger to stop her. "And that whole time he got over to the shop to see you, though, didn't he? He came running any time you had a problem at the bank, didn't he?" She replaced her pointing finger with an escalating tone, like that of a disappointed parent. "Did your taxes for YOU every year. Ran across town to fetch YOU food to save YOU money and make sure YOU had all your special favorites. Let YOU sleep in HIS bed when YOU wanna get sideways and feel sorry for yourself."

"Gia, I-"

"And I'ma guess that right now, the reason he ain't here is to make sure YOU slept okay, and so YOU could wake up with some dignity. To put YOURSELF together while he's out there in twenty degrees making sure YOU have what YOU need. So YOU can go do what YOU got to do today, right?" Gia grabbed a grocery bag off the table and closed the gap between them in the room, offering it to Tanya as she did. "But you're right, though. He ought to find a way to put into WORDS that he cares about you."

Tanya's face was hot and surely flushed if what was left of her makeup wasn't hiding it. She looked down at the bag. "What's this?"

"A slice of humble pie, honey," Gia grinned smugly. "You're gonna come get in my car, text him to find out where he is, and I'ma take you to him so YOU can take credit for the breakfast I brought him so maybe he'll be able to eat while it's still warm." Gia sighed and shook her head with a long sigh. "Hey, nobody needs to tell you that Gilly is a good guy. You ought to know better than anyone. I'm not even saying you have to date my brother. But it would mean the world to him if you'd show some appreciation before he starts to think you just use him for favors."

Tanya sheepishly took the bag and looked up with glassy eyes. "Is that what you... Is that what he thinks?"

"It only matters what I think if what I just said is true. And you know he'd never say that to me, because then I'd have had to come find you to get up in your business about it. And we wouldn't want that, would we?" Gia grabbed her purse and pulled the strap over her shoulder. "Right now I'm just trying to deliver a little thanks to my geek brother so I ain't got to use words that might give him a big head. Take notes, honey. You ain't gotta tell a man to show him."

Gia walked to the door, zipping up her white, hooded puffer coat, and clicked the lock into place on the knob as she waited. Tanya scooped up her red parka and purse and followed.

19

"Hey, Gia," Tanya bit her lip when they were in the hallway and the door was closed. "Um, thanks."

Gia grinned and cocked an eyebrow. "Thanks for what?"

***

Blake peeked through the blinds of his office window when he heard two vehicles come onto the lot. One was a tow truck hauling a convertible and the other was a similarly small car with tinted windows whose stereo bass was thumping loud enough to rattle its windows.

He finished rolling the sleeve of his grease-streaked shirt and stepped out into the cold. Blake watched as Mo parked and climbed out to address the wrecker driver and put something back into his wallet. Mo looked back to see Blake and walked over with his hands in his pockets.

"Ain't it a little early for tamales?" Blake quipped.

Mo stepped close and puffed out his chest, looking up at Blake's face. "Only an uncultured gringo would think it's ever a bad time for tamales."

A long, quiet moment passed as they stared unflinchingly at each other.

When Mo pulled a hand from his pocket, Blake met it with his own and bumped fists before the two quickly embraced.

"Where the hell have you been?" Blake asked with a laugh.

His expression changed abruptly into feigned sadness, complete with a quivering lip. "You never call or write. I was starting to think maybe you overfilled your white friend quota and had to replace me."

Mo kept a straight face. "I did, but I have to keep you in case I need job references."

They both laughed as Blake opened the office door and showed Mo inside.

"Looks like you made a new friend, recently," Mo joked, tapping a finger to his nose.

Blake smoothed the heavy tape over his nose and caught a glance of himself in the reflection of his garage window. He stepped behind his desk and sat down. "It was just a misunderstanding with a coworker. I trusted him too much and he did something stupid. Wasn't anything personal, just rookie stuff," Blake told him. "The swelling went down pretty quickly, but these black eyes look like hell. Guess I won't be winning any beauty pageants this week. Have a seat. What's up with the car?"

"I tried to jump it, but it needs a new battery," Mo replied. "I already used the free replacement on my card for my sister's ride, so I figured I'd give you the business."

Blake spread his arms and looked around at the motorcycle posters and calendar on his walls. "You know I usually work on bikes. I'm not saying I can't do it. But you must have something else on your mind to bring it here?"

21

Mo nodded, "It's Tanya's car. She's been digging up the past again. And I just keep saying all the wrong things, you know?"

Blake leaned over the desk and brushed his knuckles across his beard stubble. "And you think I can talk some sense into her? The guy who sat up drinking with her the night she lost her sister?"

Mo stood up and looked out at the tow truck leaving the lot. "No, probably not. But last night she brought up your brother a couple of times. Said any time she sees a full moon, she can't help but wonder what he's up to. And I just thought maybe-"

"You thought I was the next best thing," Blake finished the sentence. "Well, ain't that sweet? You really know how to pay a guy a compliment."

Mo rolled his shoulders, gave a long blink, and tried to keep himself calm. "What I'm trying to say is, I don't know how to reach Simon and I thought you might. That maybe you'd know how to find him by the time she comes to get her car back."

Blake pulled the top drawer of his desk open and produced a pack of cigarettes, from which he drew and lit one. He tossed the pack and lighter on the desk and pushed an ashtray out from behind the keyboard of his desktop computer.

"I haven't seen Simon in a long while," Blake said through a cloud of smoke. "His phone has been off even longer than that. Pretty much ever since my last court date, I haven't even heard from Tanya. Or you, for that matter."

"Yeah, sorry man," Mo apologized. "I've had to wear a lot of hats lately. After putting myself through school it's mostly just juggling bills and family and-"

Blake cut him off. "How is Gianna? I should see if she can check up on this bruising."

Mo grinned with a shake of his head. "She's a little out of your age bracket, ain't she? Anyway, I thought you already struck out?"

"You don't watch much baseball. One at-bat doesn't mean much in the grand scheme of things. Just got to get my timing down." He blew another long blast of smoke and showed a crooked, cocky smile.

Blake jumped up from his chair and smashed out his cigarette, looking through the blinds. "Looks like I'm on deck."

Mo spun around to follow Blake's gaze. Both men looked out at Gia pulling her car into the lot, along with a blonde passenger that must have been Tanya.

"Help me get the car into the bay real quick," Blake said. "If she's planning to wait for a battery replacement, I'd better get started. You steer, I'll push."

Chapter Four - Chicks Dig Scars

Tanya rifled through her purse for her keys and registration card while Blake drummed information into his computer.

Without looking up from the screen he told her, "I have the battery on a charger just so I can start it. I want to see if there's anything else it needs before I send you out in the cold to break down again."

Tanya nodded awkwardly and looked over her shoulder to see Mo and Gia in the parking lot talking in his car. "I'm sure everybody says this, but just whatever it needs to get going. I don't have a lot to spend on this car. If it's more than a battery, I might be better off trying to replace the whole thing."

Tanya looked up at the motorcycle calendar behind the desk, noting the model's smoldering expression and matching red hoop earrings and bikini as she sat backwards on a custom bike. The office reeked of cigarette smoke and motor oil. "Do you think I should wait, or can you just give me a call when you have an estimate?"

Blake turned the screen around so she could see. "A new battery is gonna be at least two hundred, labor included." He emphasized, "And that's IF that's all it needs. I'll have to order one since I usually only service bikes here. Even with a quick delivery, that's at least two hours."

"Um, I think I better let you do your thing and wait for your call," Tanya said. "Especially since I already have a ride here waiting."

Blake stood up and opened the office door for her. "Fine by me. You got my card in case you want to hunt the parts down yourself or change your mind about me doing the work. Short and sweet, like always, huh?"

"Uh, yeah, I guess," she answered, looking at Mo's car again. "Can't say you've changed much either, Mr. Gentry." She looked him in the eyes for the first time since arriving. "I hope whoever gave you those shiners got something in return." She stood up on her toes and kissed his cheek. "I'll be back either way, okay? Keep the bill cheap for me, will ya?"

He narrowed his eyes. "As long as the rest of your payment is in cash. Sugar don't pay my bills here."

"You must be losing your touch, then," Tanya dragged a finger along the scar at the edge of his beard.

She stopped as she spotted some kind of animal running into the nearby alleyway, hoping to get a better look at it. She walked out into the lot to see if it was still there. She sighed disappointedly, just before Mo startled her with a tap on her shoulder.

"Hey, did you sleep alright? Gia said she woke you up making noise in the apartment." He shoved his hands into his pockets and gave her some space.

"I'm fine. And I brought you some breakfast," Tanya offered. "I hope it's still warm, at least. It's in your sister's car."

"No rush," Mo shrugged. "You okay? You look like you just saw a ghost."

Tanya looked back to the alley again, and then back to Mo with a shake of her head. "It's nothing. Blake said he'd call me when he has an estimate. Do you mind giving me a ride home to change and then back to the shop? Or," she reached into the kangaroo pocket of his hooded sweater for his keys attached to a lanyard. "I can drive while you eat. As thanks for you rescuing me, like always." She dangled the keys in a pendulous motion until he reached for them. She yanked them out of reach and backed away toward Gia's sedan. She pouted at him and held the keys up over her head. Her eyes followed the dangling keys and she teased with a grin.

Mo closed the gap and pinned her against the car door. His eyes were fixed on hers and the breath went out of her chest. His eyes moved from her eyes to her lips and back up before he spoke in a low voice, "I waited this long. I can eat after I get you back to your place."

Mo backed away and reached for his keys again, which she gave easily this time. He turned to walk briskly to his car. She watched him for a moment and caught her breath with disappointment. Her heart rate wasn't even noticeable as she fiddled with her hands in frustration before turning to retrieve the food bag from Gia's passenger seat. She plucked her phone from her purse and punched a few keys to text Gia a thank you for the ride just as Mo pulled his car over close to save Tanya the walk.

***

Blake watched as Gianna circled him to get closer as he turned the key. The only sound was a click and he shook his head.

"For the first time in a long time, I have a beautiful woman and an empty backseat," he said. "What do you think? You gonna hang around a little while?"

Gia laughed and the garage echoed it back. "I don't think so. I don't know what goes on in this girl's car! Besides, I thought you were better than that. Not once have you asked properly for a date. Are you that sure of yourself?"

Blake grinned broadly and shrugged. "I always bet on me, honey."

He turned the key back and removed it, then stood up. She didn't move away to give him room, and he found himself face to face with her. Her perfume barely cut through the greasy garage smells. Over her shoulder, he saw eyes watching him from the alley. Eyes from the face of a wolf, staring back at him.

Blake placed his hands on Gia's shoulders, rubbing with his thumbs and he spoke hesitantly. "I'll put some thought into it this time. The work helps me think." He stepped away from the car and carefully closed the door behind them. "I'll come up with something you can't resist. And I'll make sure I don't have these bruised eyes when I do."

Gia curled her lip into a partial smile and crossed her arms. "Mr. Blake Gentry, for the first time, I think I'm actually curious what you might say next. So call me when you get it figured out, don't text. And don't worry about the bruises. I'm used to seeing you a little beat up when we cross paths."

She noticed who he was looking at and took a step back. "Someone you know? Is he okay out here without a coat?"

"It's an old friend, but you better go." Blake escorted her to her car without another word and patted the roof once she was inside.

He looked again to see Simon standing in the cold with folded arms in worn jeans and a tattered T-shirt. Blake held the door to the office.

Simon, once inside, went straight to a half-full coffee pot and wrapped his hands around the glass. His shirt and hair were both soaked. His face dripped with sweat and he took the pot and drank what was left in it straight from the spout. He wiped his mouth with the short sleeve of his shirt and turned to face Blake. Simon's face was sagging with fatigue. His eyes were barely open and he swayed in place as he stood.

"Help yourself," Blake offered sarcastically. "What are you doing here?"

Simon shook his hair back out of his face and looked up at the ceiling. He stretched his arms upward and leaned back

28

until his back cracked audibly. "I'm not staying. I just needed a minute. And maybe a little money." Simon put a hand on the leather chair in front of the desk and then slumped into it. "Man, I miss clotheslines. I could use some layers for this cold. And a hot meal. Been…" His eyes closed for just a moment and he snapped himself awake and then stood up again. "Been fighting a fever for two days. It breaks every so often, but won't stay away."

Blake walked past him to his desk and opened the bottom drawer. "I have a box of crackers in here you can have. Sometimes I use the coffee machine to heat water for some quick-boiled noodles. But I don't have any cash on me." He put the box of crackers on the desktop and Simon wasted no time tearing a package open with shaky hands and devouring a few.

"You got an extra pair of coveralls, maybe?" Simon asked.

Blake shook his head and spun his desk chair out of his way to reach for another cigarette. As he lit it, Simon took the leather jacket off the hook inside the door. He put it on and hugged himself inside it as he pushed a few more crackers into his mouth. Blake took the empty coffee pot to the closet-sized bathroom to rinse and refill the decanter for the machine to start percolating. "Would you rather I make a bowl of noodle soup for you, or more coffee?"

Simon looked at Blake like he didn't understand the words and blinked hard a few times.

"Never mind," Blake said. "I'll make the noodles if you've

29

got a couple of minutes."

Simon paced in between the chair and desk, still shaking. He reached across the desk for a cigarette and lit it, taking a long, deep drag, then another, coughing each time from inhaling too long. He stared for a moment at the lit end of the cigarette before he crushed it out into his palm and then rubbed his hands together. Then he went to the window and pressed his forehead against the cool glass.

"Maybe I should have kept that nurse here," Blake said. "You need some help. Michael Laurent's place is still empty if you need somewhere to lay low. You know the place? Up near the golf course? The power's out and there's no food there, but there are still plenty of clothes and things in the closets if you need them." Blake took the half pot of hot water and added a package of noodles to it in a large thermos. He added the seasoning and screwed the lid on to shake it up before Simon took it from his hands.

Simon nodded. "Yeah, I know the place. That might work." He unscrewed the lid and drank, slurping the noodles as steaming, barely mixed soup leaked from the corners of his mouth over his beard and shirt. He choked and sputtered until he couldn't take anymore and replaced the lid.

Blake finished his cigarette and stamped it out in the ashtray as Simon pressed his head against the cold window again. "I think there's a key to the house in the breast pocket of that jacket you're wearing-" His words were interrupted by the door opening suddenly. He turned to see Simon running off across the parking lot and into the alley where Blake first spotted him.

"Hell of a morning," Blake huffed as he took the coffee pot to rinse and refill again.

Chapter Five - Old Dogs

Simon's legs were too weak to keep running and he scratched all over his chest and belly as if a rash had taken over his torso. He groaned and dropped to his knees as he looked around to get his bearings. He bent over in pain and heaved, expelling the soup Blake had given to him not long ago. He was deep into the woods again. He wiped his mouth on the sleeve of Blake's jacket and fought to keep his eyes open.

The wind blew so hard between the leafless tree branches that he held up a hand over his face to block it. With it came the whispering again. Those incoherent, chilling whispers that goaded him to come further.

He looked over his shoulder, but now in his tired haze, the trees and snow-dusted earth all looked and smelled the same to him. He looked up to see that the moon in the morning sky was still visible, but just barely. Simon knelt with his arms out at his sides and allowed his eyes to close. He felt the lingering whispers grow closer, circling in and disorienting him.

Flashing images flickered behind his eyelids, each taunting the beast within him to come out and take over. Simon fought and clenched every muscle as he tried to hold on and resist the urge to give in and let himself turn.

Simon doubled over and felt the whispers touch his skin and pull in every which direction until he attempted to resist. His limbs felt heavy. He swung out and tried to stand, but the world around him now had changed. His sweat beaded and ran uncontrollably as he fought and pushed himself deeper into a mist that tapestried the air like webs. The vaporous webbing was thick and clung to him even as he tore through it. He couldn't see the trees or snow anymore but caught sight of a clear space beyond this maze of webs. The opening made his chest thrum with warmth with each step closer. Simon let loose a scream of desperation as he mustered the strength to rip through into the clearing.

Once more, he found himself out of breath and his eyes sore from staving off rest. He could see the woods again, but the trees swayed out of sync with the wind. He heard it carrying a voice and now, somehow, saw it rushing toward him. The approaching gust sang a piteous, howling stream of notes and passed him by, careful to avoid touching him as if politely sidling through a grocery aisle.

Simon pulled at the trunk of a thin tree to help him stand and the trunk bent away from him as he held on until he was on his feet. He leaned on a round knot to stop himself from falling forward, and after a moment, felt a gnawing sensation in his palm that began to tear the skin. Simon yanked his hand away to see a thorn-toothed maw chomping within the knot before the tree began to lean toward him. Simon noticed the branches above were reaching out over him like arms to pull him back. Other trees began to do the same and tried to catch him before he ran from them toward a meadow that swirled with drifts of powdery snow.

The previous whispers were now met with a kind of

murmuring, which drew Simon's attention to the nearby river. The water flowed by silently but a light shone up from under the surface near the edge, like some sort of orb was caught there and unable to make its way out onto land. When he knelt down closer, the orb emitted a brighter light and floated up toward him, close to his face. This tiny, moon-like object moved through Simon's chest and quickly flew to a large, smooth stone where it pulsed with a brighter glow.

Simon shielded his tired eyes until the flickering ceased. Where the orb had stopped was now a person, or something like one, sitting but bent over, with a wave of black hair hanging over their face.

"I don't know how long it's been," came a low echoing voice. "But I'm glad you finally heard me. I've been calling out for ages any time I could sense you were close."

Simon moved closer, blinking hard several times to be sure he was truly seeing this for himself and not dreaming. He tried to place a hand on the shoulder of the young man sitting there but it passed through. "Joshua?"

The sitting man looked up suddenly, revealing his horrific, disfigured face. Thorns and brambles were protruding where his brows, mustache, and beard hair should be. His eyes were a blazingly bright blue. He stood quickly and a familiar devilish smile spread across his face.

"I knew if anyone would hear me, it would be you," Joshua said. He licked across his lips as though they were dry before he settled to a more calm, almost lifeless expression. "I had to show you this place," he explained. "I don't think I can cross back over. I've tried so many times. I keep getting pulled back to the river. Back where I can still hear Mama sing to me."

Simon walked around this phantom of his packmate in a circle, looking him over and taking in what had changed about him. His slightly elongated features. His cold but fiery glow. Simon looked again into his old friend's unnatural eyes and asked, "Am I safe here?"

Joshua howled with maddened laughter. His face contorted as if he were in pain from his amusement. "As safe as you could ever be."

Simon looked at his hand to see the palm had already healed and he felt no pain. He pressed the same hand against his forehead. For the first time in many days, he wasn't soaked in sweat or fighting a fever. "I- I just need to rest. And then I need to go back and find the others. Can I bring them here?"

Joshua closed his eyes and began to fade out of sight. "Bring them to the river," he whispered. "I'll be waiting to show them the way."

When Joshua disappeared, Simon moved to sit on the large stone and lay back to look up at the moon beaming down over the clearing.

***

Blake wiped his hands on a towel as he crooked his neck to hold his cell phone to his shoulder. "No one ever answers their phone," he muttered impatiently as he waited for the voicemail tone. He put on his exaggerated customer-friendly voice. "Miss Johnston, your vehicle is ready to pick up at your convenience. New starter and battery, plus an overdue oil change. You'll have to take your car to another location for your inspection when it's due next month. We can settle the bill over the phone or you can stop by during regular business hours."

He ended the call just as another came in. "Whiskey Throttle Power Sports. How can I help you?" He was already shaking his head as he sat down with a pen hovering over his desktop calendar. "Ma'am, this shop handles motorcycles and other small recreational vehicles," he answered. "I understand. Yes, I'm sure a lot of places are booked up right after the holidays, but-" The familiar voice cut him short. "Alright, yes. Uh, tell you what, let me get your name and see what appointment I can make here for you."

Blake sat up straight as he stared at the name he had written and he didn't answer back right away. "Right, Von Croy you say? And, uh, what's the best number where I can reach you? Okay, thank you. We've got a good bit lined up here for the next couple of weeks, ourselves," he lied as he looked into the mostly empty garage bay where Tanya's car and a couple of dirt bikes were parked. "So tentatively we'd be looking at the end of the month, but I really don't have parts in stock for most regular cars. Right. Yes, that would mean it'd be a bit more expensive getting out of our wheelhouse, here. Mm-hmm. Tell you what, Miss Croy-"

She cut him off again to correct him. Blake cleared his throat and kept up his customer service voice. She didn't give any notion that she knew who she was speaking to. He glared at the pen, knowing he wasn't going to take any appointment from his mother. "I apologize, Mrs. Von Croy. Let me give you a ring back on Friday so our crew here can see what we can shuffle around to fit you in. But just being honest, it won't hurt my feelings if you find another place that'll save you some money, alright? Alright then, we'll be in touch by Friday. Thank you."

He had barely ended the call when a loud motorcycle pulled into the lot. "So much for an easy day," he said as he stood and poured another cup of coffee.

The sound of the engine cut out and a tall man dismounted. He was heavily bundled beneath his leathers and wore a red helmet with a black scorpion silhouette on the side. The man's gloved hands stretched out at his sides and steam blasted out through the vented mouth. The leather jacket had a series of patches on either side of the chest, and a broad banner on the back that read REGULATORS.

When the man came through the door, he pulled off his helmet and placed it in the empty chair. "I come all this way to see you, and you can't even give a warm welcome?"

Blake set his coffee mug on the desk and hugged the man tightly. "Hell, I should have known it was you right off. The only guy I know crazy enough to ride in January. And across the country? Did I read that patch right? Your MC chapter is out of Phoenix?"

"That's right, brother," the man answered and unzipped his jacket for comfort. "If DX can't ride, DX don't go."

"Speaking of going, there's something you should know if you plan on hanging around, Deacon," Blake said as he lifted his foot to the edge of his desk. He pulled up his pant sleeve a few inches to reveal an ankle bracelet monitor. "You're here as a customer, or as an employee if one of my new friends in blue comes poking around. Probation has its restrictions."

"You never were good at greetings," Deacon laughed. He took off his gloves and folded them over his belt. He pulled a braid of black hair out of the collar of his coat to let it hang free. A red and black scorpion tattoo that resembled the picture on his helmet could be seen on the shaved side of his head curled around his right ear.

"Last time I saw you, that was just a short mohawk," Blake pointed to Deacon's hair. "And you were just a skinny kid. Now you're getting a belly on you."

Deacon pulled up his shirt and sweater layers to reveal a barreled belly with a tattoo that read XAVIER in an arch over his navel. There was a small round scar just over the X and a long line scar that almost underlined the ER of his name ink. "That's all muscle. Them pretty boy abs you like don't help with the heavy lifting. Not to mention that bulk may have saved my life," he said, tickling the small round scar.

Blake let down his leg and took another drink of coffee, then gestured with his mug. "You need a warmer? I don't have anything stronger here, but it helps with the cold."

"If you made it, no thanks," Deacon declined. "I came out here to see if you'd come back to Arizona with me. And I figured a phone call wouldn't be enough to convince you. How long are you on house arrest?"

Blake went to his chair and began to write on the calendar REBUILD XAVIER and drew a line to the end of the week that followed. "Pending my court date. Which also doesn't have a date set. My lawyer said time on the bracelet will count toward time served if I'm convicted. In the meantime, they send me a bill for this little piece of state-approved jewelry until they take it off."

"Did you do it?" Deacon asked as he finally sat in the other chair after moving his helmet to the desktop. His hands each wore heavy gold rings in need of a polish.

Blake put his hands out at his sides and shrugged. "I'm, uh, not at liberty to say, as my lawyer would tell me. I can, however, tell you that it was legal but complicated."

Deacon shook his head with a serious expression. "Well, then I guess you could use the extra labor. Just help me look for a room to rent or something. I'm staying until you get your walking papers. I just gotta make a call back to the table, and find a place to buy some duds to change into. What's your cash position? You good?"

Blake finished his coffee and lit a cigarette after offering one to his friend. "It's a little tight. Winter is a bad time for this kind of business. And my side job just cut back too. But I'll get there. I have other assets that are frozen until the judge makes her decision. She's not too tough, but the case hit a… dead end. The prosecutor demanded more time to comb through the details, but my guy was good enough to keep me out of lockup until they get it all done. Now they're just having a pissing contest while I'm hanging out to dry."

Deacon looked around the office and back to Blake. "I guess while I'm on the horn, I'll see what we can do about drumming up some work for us. I'm not real big on just sitting around, especially with this cold air. Gotta do something to keep moving." Deacon cracked his knuckles and slouched in his chair. "Now for the most important question. How's the action around here?"

Chapter Six - Jagged Little Chill Pill

Once again, Tanya woke up in Mo's bedroom alone. Her head pounded, her hair was a mess, and she stunk of liquor, but she was still dressed. Near the bedside table, she found her shoes and purse, the latter from which she fished out her phone to check the time. The clock read 8:47 AM. Her lock screen showed a new picture, which was of her and Mo each holding up a glass of pink liquid and laughing together. The picture was somewhat blurry. She blinked hard to confirm it was the photo and not her hangover that was the problem.

"Maybe it'll grow on me," she said quietly to herself as she gathered her belongings to leave.

Tanya went to the door to check where Mo might be when she heard water running in the bathroom. She quickly pressed her thumb across her phone screen, opening an application for a cab to meet her down the block at a convenience store and then sneaked out the apartment door.

She sent a text message to Mo to apologize for leaving, hoping he was still showering so he wouldn't hear it. She hurried down to the ground floor before slipping on her shoes and coat to go outside.

When she arrived at Whiskey Throttle, she was glad to see there were no vehicles on the lot but hers and turned to tip the driver but was fumbling to find cash. "Do you mind if I just add it through the app? I used to work for tips, so I know how it is."

The wiry-haired driver nodded behind his sunglasses and asked, "You want me to wait til your car starts before I leave?"

"Aww, thank you," she smiled. "A girl can never feel too safe."

When she turned around, she almost walked into a tall man wearing a beanie and coveralls with the name Blake stitched on the pocket. The sleeves were rolled up but showed his black sweatshirt reaching to his wrists from underneath.

"Oh! Sorry, I didn't hear you come up behind me," Tanya managed nervously. Her eyes went immediately to the scorpion claw tattooed around his ear. He blocked the morning sun just enough that she was both squinting to see but couldn't make out his facial features.

"Hey, lady, you good?" The taxi driver sounded concerned but made no effort to get out of the car.

Tanya nodded uncomfortably without turning to face the driver and let out an icy breath. "Uh, yeah. This is my mechanic, I'm all set. Thank you."

When the driver left, the man in front of Tanya turned his head to watch until he was gone and she could see it wasn't Blake at all. His skin was leathery and tanned if not naturally brown, with black eyebrows and a strong, wide chin with black stubble.

"You're not-" Tanya started to say as she took a step back from the man.

"I'm Deacon," he said as he slowly stretched out a hand toward her.

She took another careful step back and looked to see if anyone was in the shop office.

"Hey, be cool. It's my first day, I don't want to scare nobody off," Deacon said. "I'll get my own duds in a few days, I'm just wearing one of the boss' covers so I don't wreck my stuff. Come on inside, you gotta be freezing."

"I, um- I'm sorry, I didn't mean-" she stammered.

Deacon chuckled. "It's all good. I'm a big, scary dude. Used to make a good living just standing in clubs with my arms crossed. Come on, I'll get you some coffee and you can tell me why you had a cab drop you off. You here to pick up your bike?" He held open the office door and waved her inside.

"No, I'm here to get my car," she answered quickly, finally looking up at Deacon's face to see his amber-colored eyes. He was imposing and broad with a thick middle, but when he sat behind the desk, she unclenched her muscles and made herself appear more relaxed. She could see his long, braided hair and how tight the coveralls pulled on his broad shoulders when he sat.

"Okay, well, I can tell you I'm just a wrench in here, so I can't take any payments or anything. If you need to settle up, Blake should be around in a little bit. We're not even supposed to be open yet, but I like to get started early." As if he just reminded himself, he jumped up from the chair and went to pour a cup of coffee in a tiny styrofoam cup to offer to her. "Would seem rude to only serve myself. Would you like some?"

Tanya smiled at his effort and accepted the cup. "Are all of Blake's friends so big? Seems like everyone he's introduced me to is kind of a hunk. I- I mean hulk." Her face felt hot as soon as she said it and she hid her mouth with the cup as she took a careful drink.

Deacon grinned and pulled a stretched hand down over his mouth then rested his chin on his knuckles. "Birds of a feather, right? I guess it's a pretty common thing for bouncers to be big guys. Or at least it should be if you gotta handle business."

Tanya giggled in spite of herself and crossed her legs, holding her coffee in both hands so they wouldn't fidget. "Is that where you guys met Simon, too?"

Deacon sat on the edge of the desk and crossed his arms. "I don't know no Simon, but I just got back this way from Arizona, so he probably made some new pals since then. Speaking of which, you look like you had a wild night. No offense, of course," he said, looking at her disheveled hair. "You must know where a hulk like me could fit in and meet some locals. Usually I can find a rowdy bar to get a drink after work but haven't had a chance to tour the city yet."

Tanya didn't hesitate to chime in, smoothing her hair and then tying it into a messy bun. "Sounds like you need someone to guide you around." She opened her purse and dug until she found a card. "I've been meaning to check out this place for a while now, but I don't like to try new things by myself. Maybe you-" she remembered her manners and that she had just met this man. "Maybe you and Blake could come and check it out after you close up tonight. There's a password on the back. Have you ever been to a speakeasy?"

Deacon turned the card over with a quick look. "They're not really my thing. Kind of the opposite, to be honest."

Tanya took another sip of coffee and scrunched her face at the bitterness. "I'll make you a deal. If you hate it, I'll buy all your drinks wherever you want to go from there. How's that sound?"

Deacon slipped the card into his coverall pocket. "It sounds like you just asked me on a date. Are you and all YOUR friends this fast? Cause your boyfriend isn't gonna like you going to a quiet bar with some hulk."

She shook her head too fast and spilled the coffee when she put her hands up. "Oops, I should clean that up." Tanya stood and turned toward the coffee machine looking for napkins and hiding her face as it was assuredly red again. "I don't have a boyfriend. And, uh, you know, it doesn't have to be a date. I run a business not far from here, and uh, it's good to meet new people and-" she rattled off frantically, trying to find words to sound like she was an engaging and friendly person, and to play off the clumsiness of her spill. She looked up at him from her knees as she mopped up coffee. "And it's always good practice as a business owner to make new friends, right?"

Deacon knelt next to her with a roll of blue paper towels. "Whatever you want to call it, blondie. I know I'll hate it, but I can't refuse a free drink or two with a little angel like you."

Hearing that word in reference to her again took her breath away. It was also stealing her joy of the moment but made her embarrassment subside as she gathered up the napkins to look for a trash can. "I should get going," she said as she picked up her purse.

Deacon backed off to stay out of her way. "Did I do something wrong? I know I shouldn't be getting fresh with a customer, but-"

"No, no, no," Tanya answered, still shaking her head. "I'm just-" She took a breath and looked back at him from the door. "I just realized I was supposed to get my car quick because I'm gonna be late for work. Hey, Deacon, was it?"

"Yeah, that's right. I didn't get your name though," he replied.

"Well, then meet me there tonight and find out, okay?" Tanya pushed some stray hair back over her ear that was curling toward the corner of her mouth. "Take a right at the Fletcher statue by the courthouse, and it's around the back of the community center. They host art gallery events and bingo fundraisers and that kind of thing. The door is in the alley. Be there by nine, in case I forget the password."

Tanya rushed out the door toward her car, fishing for her keys until she remembered Blake said they were in the ignition and threw the strap up over her shoulder. "Nice going, T! Run out on one guy you know is safe and trustworthy, then ask out a COMPLETE stranger within the hour. What are you even doing?"

***

When Blake came around the corner to the office door he noticed the car on the lot was gone. He set a bag on the desk and nodded as Deacon came out from the bathroom.

"I've taken buses with bigger cans," Deacon remarked as he tossed a paper towel into the trash bin.

Blake gave him a pointed look. "I thought we agreed not to discuss your exes?"

"Alright, alright. I walked into that one," Deacon laughed.

"And I bet it only took getting a good look at you under bright lights for her to walk out," Blake finished. "Speaking of women, did the owner of that car come in, or just hop in and drive off?"

"That tiny blonde? She just left. Hung out a minute and asked me out for a drink," Deacon answered with a smug grin. "Though I'm probably playing second fiddle, for now. She looked and smelled like she just came off a wild date night."

Blake squished his face in disbelief. "Tanya asked you out?

Tell me another one. She's about as touchable as Eliot Ness. Besides, I thought you'd know better than to be driving off customers by hitting on them."

Deacon threw up his hands. "Hey, hold up. I said she asked me, brother. I was just trying to stall 'til you got back so she could pay. I probably should learn how to handle that. I didn't see a cash box anywhere or a receipt book. Are you even running legit here?"

"Not that she needed to," Blake started as he pulled open a drawer. He lifted out a cash tray and a receipt book. He shook his head and marked her receipt as paid, to relieve her of the problem, and Deacon of the mistake. "Her account is all set, otherwise the keys woulda been on the rack." He looked down at the desk and added, "You must have been looking somewhere else, I guess."

"Alright, whatever. She's easy on the eyes," Deacon admitted. "You know about this place she asked me to?" He fished the card from his pocket and flicked it onto the desk.

"I don't think I need to remind you why I don't get out much," Blake said as he picked up the card and looked it over. "Looks like a new place, though, or just one that doesn't advertise." Blake sat at the desk to put the tray and book back into the drawer and cued up the computer screen.

Deacon adjusted his sleeves and slumped into the chair. "She said it was a speakeasy. One of them trending yuppy bars where you only get in if you know somebody or have a password. Twenty dollars for half-glass cocktails in a stuffy room where everybody sits on their phones and pretends that they're important."

"The kind of place where you'd stand out like a sore thumb, Deac," Blake warned.

"One step ahead. I told her I don't belong there but she said she was buying," Deacon replied. "But it's two birds with one stone, right? I get to have a look around, and I don't have to do it alone. What did you mean by untouchable? Is that some kind of challenge?"

"No!" he laughed. "Definitely not. It's just I've kind of kept an eye on her for a while," Blake explained as his face became serious. "She's a friend of mine. She only gets shy when someone shows interest. And only seems interested in guys that aren't into her. She's like a feral stray cat. She'll eat if you open a can, but it ain't gonna be your pet."

Deacon put his feet up on the desk and crossed them as he folded his hands behind his head. "Good people rescue strays every day, brother."

"Well, when you see a good person, let me know. I'll give him her number." Blake stood up to look out the window. "Hey, have some of the breakfast I brought back from next door. I got something to take care of outside."

Blake walked out into the cold before a police patrol car came to a stop on the lot, and the driver rolled the window down with a condescending look.

"You were out of bounds a couple of minutes ago. I've already given you a warning," the officer said. A cruel smile stretched his lips. "I ought to just bust you right here, but I can see you're so busy that I'm sure I'll be back for you when your fines don't get paid."

As the cruiser pulled away Blake muttered, "It's not a fine, it's an equipment rental fee." He shrugged away the cold and returned to the office to find the bag on the desk was empty, and the trash can was nearly full.

Deacon added another wet paper towel to the trash. "Sorry, bro. I'll go get you another sandwich."

"Forget it," Blake shook his head. "Lost my appetite. We got a snowmobile coming in around eleven, that'll give us some time to look over those dirt bikes to keep us busy."

Chapter Seven - Don't Hand Me No Lines

The car door opened and a well-dressed man stood holding it with his hand out to help Melissa from the limousine. "Welcome! We've all been eager to meet you formally."

Melissa refused his hand and stepped out of the limousine unassisted, wearing a wispy, black evening dress with matching mid-heels. She walked through a crowd of excited people who eagerly made way for her. They stood with glasses of champagne raised, awaiting the signal to complete a toast they had begun in anticipation of her arrival.

"I'm Adam Solomon, and this is my home," the man who held the door announced. "I trust Mr. Christian already informed you that we gathered here to welcome-"

Melissa turned back to Solomon with a cold, fixed gaze. "You shouldn't trust such a man, Mr. Solomon. Your chaperone put his hands on me without my permission." She spoke clearly so the gathering of people could hear. "I spared his life as a warning to him, you, and your guests, that my company here at YOUR request is entirely upon MY own terms. Do we understand each other?"

Without waiting for an answer, she turned to walk through the manicured courtyard and immense, ornate, wooden double doors of the mansion that awaited her.

Solomon had caught up to her once she was inside and

51

offered her a flute of champagne, which she waved away without looking at him. "Is this any way to begin our relationship? Killing a man who-"

"He's not dead, Mr. Solomon," she cut in calmly. "Though he should be, and very well may be without appropriate attention." Melissa turned to face him, looking him over thoroughly. "You care too much about your appearance for a man who can buy attention. Dying the gray out of your carefully clipped pompadour. Clean-shaven in the dead of winter but have no company to represent in front of your shareholders."

Solomon attempted a quiet laugh but was not allowed to respond as she went on.

"You're wearing a tuxedo from a designer no one can afford. The coat length is a bit long for your corded stature to attempt a perception of being taller than you are, as if anyone wouldn't notice you wear heeled boots to do so. A silk ascot as opposed to a simple, elegant bow tie seems like a style choice. But clearly, it's just another piece to make you stand out and allows you to show off a piece of unnecessary jewelry in the form of a clasp, custom-made if I'm not mistaken, from a cheaper metal like the kind used to make military identification tags. You spared no expense on material, but cut costs on your tailor, as your sleeves are too short, which even you notice by the way you keep one arm bent and the other hand in your pocket."

Solomon cleared his throat politely and began to walk toward a table on one side of the room. When she appeared suddenly in his way, it elicited a double take from him to where she had just been standing.

Melissa circled him like a vulture as the crowd found their way into the main hall to join them. "You have money and a lot of it. Rich but not wealthy, which means you can get it but haven't quite learned how to spend it. That accounts for this immense, mostly unfurnished home in the hills off of an unpaved back road in one of the most uninteresting places in the world. So you must have some kind of personal ties to the area but don't wish to engage directly with them and prefer to make others come to you. Your backyard is a country club that requires overpriced membership and dress codes and arrogantly has no prices on their dining menu. No doubt, occupied by your acquaintances," she gestured to the quiet mob of guests. "Those who have names that look like top-shelf liquor labels or microwavable gourmet TV dinners. Shall I go on, Mr. Solomon?"

Solomon lifted his brows and addressed his guests with a look of being impressed. "I just knew I was going to enjoy your company the moment I laid eyes on you. I'd like to properly introduce you, but I haven't had the pleasure of your name."

"Your pleasure is not why you asked me here," Melissa accused. "You want me here because you've found something you can't break. Something that makes your upper lip sweat. Something that makes your skin crawl. And because you're not afraid of it, you're intrigued by the challenge." She turned from him and stepped closer again to the gathering of people. Their excitement had turned to fear as they continued to glibly hold onto their glasses without yet taking a drink.

"Which for now, is the only quality you have that I admire. It will not serve you to pursue that interest. I do not belong to you. Consider my fee to be that of a celebrity appearance without an expiration date. Do we understand each other?"

Solomon boasted a proud, white, toothy smile to Melissa and then to his guests with a nod. "I couldn't be happier to have you here as an honored guest in my home. May I?" he asked, taking her hand to kiss it. "I can learn a lot from you, I'm sure. I can't wait to get started."

He raised her hand in his, presenting her to the others. He finally raised his glass again and his guests did the same before they all drank to Melissa and applauded.

***

Tanya locked the shop door early and chose a few items from the racks to try on. She checked her phone for a weather update, slipped on a pair of flat boots that covered the legs of her skinny jeans, and adjusted a large sweater that kept slipping off of one shoulder. She switched her purse contents to a larger, leather tote that had a variety of internal compartments. She reserved this bag for nights when she went out hunting leads on Melissa. Tucked to one side, she checked that the safety was set on the light handgun and that a large pocket above it still held a pair of capped syringes.

With another look at the time, she hurried out the door to her car and shared a guilty stare with herself in the mirror as the car hummed to life without any trouble. She let out a sigh that steamed the mirror and windshield slightly and then tried to steel herself. A slow-moving car behind her in the lot intensified her grip on the steering wheel and she couldn't relax until the driver moved on.

She took the drive carefully. Once parked, she took a few minutes to double-check her eye makeup and sprayed a sweet-smelling mist before exiting the car.

Tanya approached a plain, heavy service door behind the Fletcher Community Center and entered before she could talk herself out of staying. Inside was a hallway that smelled faintly of bleach and the walls held pieces of art donated from the local historical society. A body-length mirror hung from one wall where she hesitated for a moment when the door behind her opened.

A handsome but slightly chubby man walked toward her, leading with a hooked nose as he buttoned his blue blazer. He ran his fingers over his slick, black hair and approached Tanya closely. His breath smelled of booze, but he appeared to be composed. "Having trouble getting in?"

Tanya tightened the strap on her tote purse across her shoulder and rested her hand over the opening.

"Whoa, no need for that," he raised his hands and stepped back, showing an impressed and amused smile. "I'm just here for a drink. Name's Riff."

Tanya pushed her purse back on her hip and pulled a tube of lip gloss to apply with a smug grin. She crossed her arms and shifted her weight to one side. "Riff? Is that short for something?"

"It's what my friends call me," he replied, lowering his arms. "Are you waiting for someone, or did you forget the password?"

Tanya paused and dipped her chin. "I lost my card. I had the password scribbled on the back and could hardly read it anyway. Maybe you could help a girl out?"

Riff laughed and adjusted a garish gold ring on his pinky finger. "I can do better than that. Let me buy you a drink to apologize for coming on stronger than a two-dollar cologne, huh?" He leaned against the wall and knocked twice. When a matching knock came back, Riff answered, "Jaded."

The wall with the mirror pulled back and they were greeted by a stunning, voluptuous woman with cupid-bow lips that bore a bright, glittery shade of purple lipstick, and a wave of canary yellow hair over one eye. She pulled her cat-eye glasses down her nose and winked at Riff. "Welcome back, sweet-cheeks. I see you found a friend. Guess I'll have to keep my hands to myself tonight." She wore a pin tag that read "Camille" on the cup of her spilling, black balconette bodice.

Riff greeted her with a side hug, careful not to upset the tray in her other hand. "Don't count yourself out too quickly, Cammie. She and I just met. Won't even tell me her name. Would you set us up with a couple of Bee's Knees to help us grease the wheels?"

"Sure thing, Riff-Raff," Camille said. "Virgin or straight?"

Riff looked back at Tanya with a grin. "I haven't asked yet, but I'm hoping straight." He clicked his tongue with a wink of his own and gestured Tanya toward an empty table.

The place was standing room only at almost full capacity with some high round tables situated throughout the space. Most of the main floor was kept open to make room to mingle. The decor was that of an old train station with a brick facade and lantern sconces. The corner of the bar held a grated locomotive plow and much of the art portrayed locally run locomotive engines. Drink specials were written on a blackboard-painted section of wall above the bar with cocktail names like, "Night Train," "Full Steam," and "Rail Car."

The air inside swirled with an ever changing redolence of different flavored vape clouds that were somehow both pleasant and turning Tanya's stomach at the same time. They stopped at an unoccupied table where Tanya looked back toward the door to see if Deacon might have arrived, then remembered present company and gave Riff a polite smile. "So, Riff-Raff, you're a regular, huh?"

Riff confessed as he waved at another patron across the room. "I don't like to call myself that, but it's hard to deny. I like it here. Even when it's full, it never gets too loud. Makes it easier to talk to people and know your drink order was heard. So, how did you hear about this place?"

Tanya reached into her purse and produced one of her business cards to place on the table. "I have a little clothing store called Second Skin. I take in donated outfits and alter them to keep current with newer fashions for an affordable price. Someone dropped off a big box of attic clothes that were in great shape and told me I should check out this place."

"Oh, a business owner. Good for you! Tanya Johnston," he read. "I like that. I don't know no Tanyas. Very nice. Never know who you're going to meet while building a brand, right? Are you doing well?"

Tanya made an unsure face and fiddled with her purse strap. "I'm in the black. I've got an incredible accountant who keeps me from running things out of pocket. It's all in who you know, they say."

Camille delivered their gold-colored drinks in coupe glasses with lemon twist garnishes and lingered a moment when she spotted the business card. "You're Second Skin? Ooh-la-la! I've been meaning to get over there. Finding things I like in my size is such a chore! And it kills my bank account!" Camille admitted. "It says here you do on-site alterations. Do you think you could hook a girl up? I need to up my game if I want a chance at competing with dolls like you!" She playfully nudged Tanya with an elbow.

"I'm sure I can get you into something that suits your style and turns heads," Tanya said, hearing her shop voice come out instinctively. She reached for her purse and fanned-out a short stack of cards on the table. "Our hours are on the card, and if you want to help me spread the word I can get you more. I'll throw in a free fitting for you when you bring a friend to shop."

"Stellar!" Camille almost shouted. "I better keep moving. Enjoy your drinks. MWAH!"

Riff looked on at how Tanya handled herself and lifted his glass. "If you'd like to make some more connections, I know a few local owners who are great assets in getting referrals and positive cash flow. Just like you said, it's all in who you know."

Tanya looked up at the door again, checked her phone, then returned her gaze to Riff and lifted her glass. "To new friends?"

Riff clinked his glass against hers and emptied his glass in one swallow. "I'm glad you agree. Let's go!"
"Wait, what?" Tanya was taken aback. "We just got here."

Riff offered his hand. "I hear you. But it just so happens I was pregaming for a little party with these people. Opportunity doesn't always knock twice. Take a chance."

"You don't take no for an answer, do you?" Tanya asked, smiling despite herself. "You owe me another drink when we get there." She downed her drink also, noting the bite of too much gin that curled her lips under her teeth.

Riff laughed loudly and took her hand. "Hey! That's the spirit!"

Chapter Eight - Par for the Course

Simon had to keep himself focused on tracking the pack. He couldn't help but feel his senses restored and sharpened after resting and meeting with, who he now knew to be, Joshua. He had picked up their scent and some tracks through the woods and noted that Mama had smartly been marking her path. They were circling back toward Joshua's burial site but he hadn't seen or smelled any signs of Sam.

He chose to hurry himself in a straight line for the goal and morphed into his four-legged wolf form to go even faster and better combat the cold.

Once the wind had picked up, he caught the strong scent of Fisher who soon paired up beside him to join the run. They briskly closed the last couple of miles and finally returned to two-legged humans when they heard the voices of Reno and Mama arguing over needing a new meeting place. Just before turning the corner of the dilapidated cabin, Simon and Fisher both took note of vomit near the crumbling porch and shared a look.

Fisher broke in between the two to announce, "Look what I found!" He straightened what was left of his torn t-shirt and hugged his thin frame against the night air.

Simon took off his borrowed leather jacket and offered it to Fisher as the four of them came closer together. "I'm guessing you guys figured out we've been running from shadows?"

Reno huffed heavily and made a gesture of apology. "I knew I was fighting it. It gets the better of me more than I'd like to admit."

Simon put up his hands and enjoyed a long draw of the air after his run. "We all know how it is. And how rough it's been lately. But I need to show you all something that I think will help smooth things over. Where's Sam?" He noticed all of them were in frayed clothing. They were shifting from foot to foot and rubbing their hands and arms for warmth.

Mama tried to blink away a tired expression. "We were just about to circle back around and see if we missed her. Her scent is strong, so she's been here recently. With us all here together, it's hard for Mama's nose to tell her babies apart." Mama held out her arms and tightly embraced Simon and Fisher together.

Something inside the cabin crashed and the back door flung open. They watched Sam run out from the back door and double over near a tree where she wretched violently. Mama let go of the two men and rushed over to check on the young woman.

Reno had begun to pace again like he had before with growing impatience. He rolled his neck and turned toward Simon. The shadowy darkness hid his expression as he approached. "Whatever it is you think will help, I think we could use a win right about now."

Simon nodded and pulled his hair into a twist. "Everybody should hunt if you haven't already. Get your guts in check. Meet back up by the river where we split up before. You're gonna feel that tug again, I'm sure. But rail against it and be there by midnight. It would be best for you to each take one of the girls and keep them apart until then." He motioned for both men to come closer. "I have reason to believe Samantha is most likely pregnant, which-" he began, keeping their attention with a calm tone. "Which will be a new challenge for us all, but we need to treat her delicately and positively. It could be at least part of the reason we've all been having high anxiety. Her scent has changed, their cycles aren't synced. And our being on the run isn't helping anyone." Simon gave Reno a serious look, and told him frankly, "Reno, you could probably use some space. See you at midnight."

Reno reluctantly nodded but didn't argue and took another look at the women huddled together. He stretched to crack his knuckles and back, then ran off into the dark woods on four legs.

"You really think her pregnancy has us all messed up?" Fisher asked.

Simon reached into the pocket of the jacket Fisher wore and fetched a key to stuff into his jeans. "I can explain better when we get there. This key belongs to a safe house we can use for a while, but we'll get to that tomorrow. Take care of this jacket, I should try to return it to my brother in a couple of days once we get our heads on straight. Now," he clapped a hand on Fisher's shoulder. "Are you more comfortable with Mama or Sam?"

"I'll run with Mama. She doesn't push me around." Fisher lowered his gaze to hide the color in his cheeks.

Simon nodded with understanding. "She's young. You're young. I can do the math here." He walked over to explain to the women while Fisher waited by the cabin.

Mama let go of Sam's thick mane of red hair and helped her stand up. "Whatever you got to show us, I hope it's good, baby. We got a bun in the oven and need someplace safe and warm before this little one comes. We need to get her some care set up. It's been a long time, but I think I can handle a delivery. Oh, but that's months and months away."

Simon looked between the worried expressions of both women. "Let's take a breath, okay? Sam, I'd like you to come with me, and Mama to go with Fisher. With everybody so tense lately, I think it's the best way to get through the next hour or so. And Mama, make sure Fisher behaves." He leaned down and placed a kiss on Mama's forehead. "Midnight, okay?"

Mama grabbed Simon's neck and pulled him down to kiss his lips. "Don't you go off and leave me again, you hear? These boys need you. I need you." Mama took Sam's hand and squeezed it before walking away. "Come on, baby!" Mama called to Fisher as she wiped her watering eyes. "Mama needs a good run and you better keep up."

"What about you?" Simon asked Sam. "Are you feeling up for a hunt before midnight?"

"I had second thoughts," said Reno, returning from the darkness. His tone was threatening and his jaw was set. "I think I've done fine keeping us going while you ran off to go borrow a coat without thinking of us."

Simon stood between Reno and Sam, taking on a defensive posture. "Reno, don't."

Reno scowled. He pressed forward with a menacing look in his eyes and short of breath. "You come back in like the hero with some new solution. Something your old pal Reno was too blind to see, huh? Well, I saw you two kissing, as if anybody doesn't know you're an item. And now singling out the pup, too-"

"I'm not a pup!" Sam cut in.

"SHUT UP!" Reno spat. "Both of you, just shut up! I'm not going to be ordered around by you anymore. You're always quick to tell everyone what's best. And just as quick to run off as soon as we have a minute to breathe. You ain't pulling your weight with us. And now you think you can just come back from another one of your little sabbaticals and show us the light? It isn't always about YOU!"

"I said you needed space," Simon tried to reason. "I found a place where we can get warm and out of the woods."

"Out of our element! We're animals! Hiding out here away from your precious friends and whatever it is you do. Meanwhile, telling this girl it's not safe for her to go home. Telling us it's not safe to stray too far from the river. It's not safe to be what we are!"

Simon shot a look at Sam who had already started to run back into the cabin. Reno pushed through Simon before he morphed into his beastly form and tore through the door separating him from Sam. Simon heard crashing and breaking inside the structure and saw clouds of dust and dirt pounding free from the joints in the wood outside. A side window broke out and he could see the slender wolf form of Sam running toward the gravel road.

Simon matched Sam on four legs and ran after her, struggling to keep up. Her scent had indeed changed and the bluster of wind made it impossible to ignore. In front of him, Simon saw she had turned back toward him and now showed her hulking werewolf form bearing down on him. Simon diverted to go deeper into the woods where there were more twisted and exposed roots to slow the two beasts pursuing him.

Simon ran on, slowing his pace to lure his pursuers. The open space beyond the treeline was a sprawling country club golf course. Before he could draw them back into cover, the two beasts collided into a fairway bunker littered with dead leaves.

Simon returned to his human form and reached for his revolver, noting the cylinder only held two bullets. With careful aim at the darker and larger of the two beasts fighting each other, he fired off both rounds and tucked the gun away to bait them into a chase again.

When he rounded the corner of a darkened hilltop mansion, Simon skidded to a halt. He was too late, with Sam and Reno right behind him, to lead them away from a car coming into the driveway. He ducked down behind some hedges to miss getting caught in the headlights. With a look around the building, he saw a gathering of people through a window who were dressed in formal attire. He could see the car turn toward a back lot down a hill where at least two dozen cars were parked.

"This can't be the place Blake told me about. Who are all these people? What have I done?"

Simon ran as fast as he could toward the tree line where he could still see the house. As he passed a patio to get a better look, he could swear he saw a familiar woman in the center of the main room standing away from the others. She was facing Simon and seemed to be watching his every move like she knew he would be there.

He hesitated long enough that he almost didn't see the shadows of the werewolves behind him. He dove into the hard pavement and the two beasts crashed into the glass doors as he scrambled to find cover where he could see what would happen next. Simon looked on as this woman threw her arms out to her sides and bellowed, "ENOUGH!"

He shivered to look upon the woman as both Reno and Sam slowly climbed to their feet, ignoring a man between them who had one arm in a sling. They stood apart from each other giving their attention to this woman but frozen to the spot as if they were commanded to do so. Simon's legs felt heavy and he could feel himself staring but unable to blink.

Again, she said the word and he loosed a bated breath as his friends wavered and collapsed. Simon finally blinked and slunk backward, keeping low, and made some distance between himself and the mansion where he could keep watch out of sight.

"Melissa? Is that even possible?" he whispered to himself in disbelief.

***

The party guests had kept themselves occupied with chatter while Solomon walked Melissa around the ground floor, prattling on about the home's composition and history for what must have been at least an hour. But now their attention was back on her as she stopped in the main hall and peered outside at two large animals approaching.

Two gunshots rang out. Solomon attempted to draw her attention away from the glass patio doors. "I'm sure it's nothing to be concerned about. Some folks in the area didn't get their fill of their New Year's celebrations, perhaps."

Solomon stopped talking when he noticed her gaze and followed her eyes to see what had Melissa so captivated. He motioned for his bodyguard, the freshly bandaged Mr. Christian, to remain quietly where he was despite his duty to place himself in the way of any harm that may come to his employer.

The husky bodyguard had removed his blazer from one arm where he now wore a makeshift sling made from a kitchen apron. A square patch bandage covered a cut on the left side of his balding head. He stubbornly maintained his posture while keeping an elbow tucked tightly against his ribs to stave his discomfort.

The glass from the patio doors shattered inward. Two hulking beasts crashed through the doors in a tangle of bites and claws. The open room echoed with a series of growls and whines that incited screams of panic from the people looking on near the mansion's entrance.

Melissa stepped toward them. "ENOUGH!" she belted with her hands extended at her sides. The beasts had landed only inches from Mr. Christian as he stood his ground. They separated from each other and climbed slowly to their feet with chests heaving out of breath. "Enough."

Both of the beasts wavered in place with labored breath on weak knees. The smaller of the two toppled over, then the larger followed. Mr. Christian remained frozen with terror between their bodies until they fell and then kicked away a furry paw that had landed on his foot.

Melissa lowered her hands and a mixture of confused and excited applause took over the room until she glowered at the crowd to stop. "You'd be wise to contain these creatures before they awake, Mr. Solomon. Or maybe you'd prefer to put them out of their misery?"

The host gestured to Mr. Christian and went to speak quietly to his guests. Melissa could overhear them talking about cleaning up the mess and how to dispose of the creatures that crashed their party.

Melissa walked over to the bodies that were shrinking into a man and a woman before her eyes. Both were dressed in fraying clothing, barely more appropriate for the winter weather than her own attire. The man had closely clipped hair and a deep scar across much of his scalp, and the woman's face was covered by long, thick red hair. The crowd, too, had noticed the transformation and were muttering excitedly amongst themselves at what they had witnessed.

"My friends, if you please," Solomon beckoned. "We have some unexpected work to do. Mr. Christian, take a few men with you downstairs to empty my vault as quickly as possible. That's where we'll be housing our new arrivals until I can make other arrangements. And you folks, with me, please. We'll gather supplies to sweep up the broken glass and cover the opening from the cold."

Melissa glared at the remaining guests who stood idly by and appeared to be confused. She turned away from them to go up the stairs. When she reached the balcony above, she saw two new guests had just arrived. One was a man in a blue suit with oily hair and his date, who clung to his arm, was a familiar-looking blonde woman. She wore a thick sweater that had slipped off of one shoulder, revealing her bra strap.

Melissa didn't wait to see how they were received and chose to look into the room at the end of the walkway to see if it met her needs. The sparsely furnished room was adorned with heavy drapes at both of its windows, which she drew closed. She turned to run her fingers over the comforter on the bed before going back to check that the door had a proper, sturdy lock. It was early, but she knew it was best to make herself scarce in case her host could not properly handle the werewolf intrusion.

Chapter Nine - Another Stakeout

Tanya took Riff's arm to accept his help out of his luxury sedan. She held onto it as they walked together through the courtyard to the hilltop mansion. Once they had entered the ornately carved doors, she could see a group of people talking amongst each other. They wore formal tuxedos and evening gowns, many of which were covered with furs or overcoats. They turned to meet the late arrivals with a hush, which reminded her of being the outcast at a school dance.

Tanya sighed inwardly at her choice of clothing and put on a nervous, polite smile. She glanced over at Riff with a raised brow to cue him.

"Sorry, I forgot myself," Riff apologized. He brought Tanya farther into the room where their attention was drawn to the sound of broken glass being swept across the hard floor. A man and woman were being helped out of the room who appeared to be unconscious. "Looks like the party started without us. If you don't mind waiting for some proper introductions, I should see if they need some help." Riff took off his blue blazer and wrapped it around Tanya's shoulders before he hurried over to assist in moving the knocked-out couple.

Tanya hugged herself inside the jacket and kept the opening of her purse close at hand. One of the men in a glittery tuxedo proposed they move the group to another room. "No reason to stand here and catch a cold. Looks like the fun is over for now. Why don't we all go into the lounge for a drink and get better acquainted with Riff's new friend here?" The man had a pouf of golden, finger-combed hair that moved with his eyebrows and a shaggy mustache that may have been colored to match.

They were ushered into the next room and the door was closed behind them. An older woman in a silvery fur coat and heavy makeup gently adjusted the key switch of the cobbled fireplace to stoke the gas-fed flames. A tall, ghastly-thin man, easily into his fifties with a blond ponytail, stepped behind the wet bar in the near corner and began setting up snifters to pour brandy.

Tanya took a drink after the man insisted she do so and he introduced himself as Lanny Prichard, an investment banker originally from the Midwest. Pointing to the woman in silver fur, he told Tanya, "That's Anna May, my ex-wife. She was a three-time Miss Drumsticks before I convinced her to run away with me out here. Then she won Coal Queen two years in a row. Don't tell her, but that's practically ancient history. Now she's recently remarried for the fourth time, I think, to an art dealer who is always too busy with his yacht club in the tropics to spend time with her. His loss is our gain. The men here give her the attention she can't get on some yacht full of young party girls. Watch she doesn't get jealous with you here," he winked.

Anna May was surrounded quite comfortably by a few men who shamelessly flirted and egged on her stories of pageants from years gone by.

Lanny went on, pointing at a short man with stubby fingers who held onto a smoldering cigar. "There's Peter Wright. I'm sure you've seen his real estate billboards." He gestured with air quotes, "Wright place, Wright time, Wright price!" Lanny raised his glass as Peter heard his slogan and threw a waving hand up. "And our 'new money' there with the coat of wax on his horseshoe scalp and the little round glasses is David Sterling-"

Tanya waved her glass in Lanny's direction. "I'm sure I'll meet everyone in due time. But between a couple of drinks earlier and this one, I might have trouble remembering everyone's names. But you ought to be able to handle a new one. I'm Tanya Johnston from Second Skin." When he narrowed his eyes she filled in the blank. "It's a clothing store downtown. You probably drive past every day on your way to your office."

His expression brightened. "I guess I'm not as up-to-date as I should be. You must be doing well to get an invite to one of these soirees. Are you diversified, or just self-investing for now?"

Tanya laughed, "You work fast, Mr. Prichard. I have most of my money tied up in my own business for now, but Riff told me this was where I need to be if I want to keep from getting buried too deep."

Lanny raised his glass with a nod. "Well, he's probably right about that. Full disclosure, the people here have thrown money at some pretty dodgy ideas, myself included. There's a sort of thrill to it, not being sure all the time if things will pan out. And we're far enough from the office that your pitch doesn't have to be too polished. But we're not all business. This is where we come to have our fun, and have sort of built a trust, if you will, of little adventures that we share."

"So," Tanya pressed as she looked back at the closed door. "That mess out there, and the people who were hurt are part of your fun? Because you guys seem pretty casual about it. I shouldn't judge, being late to the party. But was there some kind of fight?"

Lanny put his arm around her and took her closer to a less crowded corner. "Oh, that was quite a surprise! Those two crashed through the patio from outside during our toast, and they were tearing each other apart. And if I'm being honest, I don't think even our purveyor, Mr. Solomon, knew anything about it. You wouldn't believe it unless you saw it yourself. He had just introduced us to this little bombshell of a woman, and these monsters," he whispered, "I think they might be werewolves, but you'd think I'm crazy." He switched back to his speaking voice to continue telling the story. "These big hairy monsters came through the patio fighting each other. And this woman, whose name we still don't know, just commands the room and stops them in their tracks. Then they collapsed into all that broken glass and this witch, or whatever she is, just handed old Solomon a piece of her mind and showed herself upstairs while they went to work cleaning up. We have no idea who those party crashers are or if we can really call them people yet." He took a long drink from his glass and finished it while his eyes rolled to one corner in thought. "It's hard to explain. Honestly, I damn near pissed myself, but I felt so drawn to this woman and whatever she was doing that I was frozen to the spot, like watching a train wreck. It might just be a product of our being a bunch of thrill-seekers. Maybe we've just set the bar too high to be surprised or scared by much."

Tanya didn't flinch at first when he mentioned werewolves and witches but forced herself to show widened eyes and respond with guarded body language as he spoke. She swirled her glass after another careful sip of her brandy, as she didn't care much for the taste. "Thrill-seekers? You mean like base jumping or bull riding?"

Lanny refilled his glass and took hers when he saw she was babying it. He pulled out a couple of bottles and made a quick martini to give back to her. "I hope that drink is a little more your speed. We've taken some sport fishing trips for marlin and tuna, which is fun for the bigger guys. We've rented out tracks and raced hot rods. Brought out all kinds of guns to shoot off while the golf course is shut down for the season. We've been talking about a big game hunt, but no one can settle on the choice of prey." He had a hungry look about him as he leaned closer and looked her over. "How fast can you run?"

Tanya caught herself mid-sip and tried to gauge his expression. "In heels or flats?" She tried to join in on his joke with a fake laugh. When Lanny returned a genuine laugh she folded her arms to rub the goosebumps, took another drink, and licked nervously at the cling of sweet vermouth on her lips.

***

When the cleanup had finished and his friends had been dragged out of sight, Simon began to scout the perimeter of the house on the hill. He saw the woman that he believed to be Melissa move toward a large staircase. He chose to hide for a moment when a new guest was welcomed through the front door, as it may have been the only distraction he would get to reposition himself.

He quickly made his way down the hill to the parking lot. Looking back up toward the house for any sign of trouble, Simon worked his way from car to car peeking through the windows for anything useful that might identify the party guests. The lingering smell of hot motor oil led him to the most recently used vehicle where he found the door unlocked and keys still in the ignition. When he opened the door, mixed odors of booze and perfume musk assaulted his nostrils. He had to shake his head to focus and quickly but quietly closed the door. The perfume was familiar, but it had been such a long time since he'd seen either of the sisters who often shared it. It confirmed his belief that he had seen the older of the two just moments ago.

Simon continued to look for safe places with a clear view of the mansion, but the golf course did not provide what he needed. Even the trees in sight were all dead and leafless. Instead, he opted to return to the edge of the grounds to wait among the more forested area, climbed high into the twisted branches of a sturdy maple, and fixed his gaze on what he could see of the house and its entry points.

He felt the uncomfortable stab of Blake's house key in his pocket and fetched it to give it a look for any indication that it belonged to the house he was watching. It was a copy and bore no helpful markings. Simon looked to the sky and morphed just his face with some effort. He howled a distressful sound toward the river where he was supposed to meet the others.

It was hours before he caught sight of Mama and Fisher coming through the woods. Simon quickly explained the mess he had made by luring their packmates to the country club mansion and why he couldn't stay.

"I need you two to keep an eye on the place from a distance," Simon explained. "It's my fault they're in this mess, but this was supposed to be the safehouse Blake told me about. I need to know why he sent me here and who these people are before we make a bad situation worse." He jumped down from the tree and stopped when he saw the disdainful look on Mama's face.

"You couldn't tell me about my Joshua?" Mama asked with a mix of emotions and pointed a stiff finger close to Simon's face. "Don't even shake your head at Mama. Don't even try to say I wouldn't believe it! When you know something, you got to tell me! And don't nobody care how damn crazy it sounds, you hear?" She pushed her hands up like a wall in between them and bit at the inside of her lips as they rolled off her teeth. "We done been through too much, and seen things that don't make no sense for you to be keeping secrets!"

"I know, Phie-" Simon started, and pulled back when Mama's eyes widened with a threatening look. "I know, Mama. I was worried about Reno. And after what happened, even though

77

it hurt you, I know it was right not to say it then. He still won't believe it until he sees for himself."

Mama put her hands down and turned away from Simon. "He- He's so different. That place is so different. Do you think it's safe to stay there? Over a longer time, I mean?" Mama asked. She turned again, looking up into his face. "Simon, I felt so free there. I didn't feel the cold. The wet, the hunger. All of it just felt lighter. But not like they were lifted off of me. More like I was lifted from those problems. And if that's where my Joshua is now, is that where we're going? Our own sort of…"

Simon reached out and pulled her close. "I thought so, too, at first. But I don't think it's any less dangerous than this place. Just different. I have to go now. Watch over each other," he said as he cast a look at Fisher who had been quietly pacing between a few sturdy trees. Fisher stretched his arms out much longer than the sleeves of the leather jacket Simon gave him and nodded back.

Simon had to give Mama a nudge to get her to let go. He wasted no time once she stepped back before turning to run off into the woods.

Chapter Ten - An Unlikely Accord

Tanya politely tried a handful of times to get away from the other guests so she could explore the mansion but was only met with refilled drinks and bragging stories disguised as business advice after Lanny had informed the entire room that she was a new business owner. She hadn't seen Riff since he offered to assist in the cleanup and she had just finally managed to excuse herself to find a restroom as a last-ditch effort to break away.

She accepted Lanny's escort to the bathroom beneath the stairs and chose to remain there until she was sure he had gone back to the lounge with the others. When she made to peek out the door, she caught sight of two men in the main hall who were discussing the break-in.

The man with the pompadour had his hands on his waist and spoke frankly to a balding man with one arm in a sling. "Mr. Christian, we're going to need to find more suitable quarters for our new beastly guests. I feel strongly that letting them go will only bring them back here in time. It's a truly amazing discovery, not unlike our Miss Johnston. Both parties are to be kept under close watch and, as you are well aware, with the utmost caution."

Tanya's eyes grew wide at the sound of her name and she stepped back from the door. She had to collect her wits and control her breathing before she could trust herself to go close enough to hear again.

The same man was still speaking when she could hear. "I've decided that since he was so bold to bring that woman into my home uninvited, the consequence of his actions will be the first watch over those who destroyed my beautiful patio."

Mr. Christian nodded. "These… guests had no sort of identification. No wallets, keys, or other effects on their person, Mr. Solomon. Their clothes were filthy and worn. Frankly, sir, they both reek. Vagrants of some kind."

"You are free to call them what they are," Solomon said, gesturing with a wave of one hand. "We've experienced folklore in the flesh tonight in a unique opportunity to study them, understand them. And, if our Mr. Prichard is still so inclined, to hunt them and more of their kind. It is incumbent on us to believe more will come looking for them. We will need to fortify our security."

Mr. Christian grinned. "Will my earlier suggestions for camera and perimeter measures be suitable, sir?"

Solomon paced, turning toward where Tanya crouched. "Yes, of course. I was mistaken to doubt you. Please see to it right away. Begin implementing the changes in the morning, if possible." He began walking toward the door where Tanya had been hiding.

Tanya couldn't help but panic at his approach. There was no other way out of the bathroom and no place in the clean and mostly empty space to hide herself. She cinched her purse strap tight where she could hide her hand inside in case there was trouble from Mr. Solomon, then knelt on the floor. She leaned over the toilet seat to feign sickness just before she heard him knocking.

He entered when she didn't answer and approached quickly with a concerned tone. "Is there anything I can get you? My parties can get carried away sometimes. I'm Adam Solomon. I know this is no way to meet, but you haven't given me much choice, have you?"

He waited patiently on one knee and brushed hair away from her face. Tanya sold her ailment by gently groaning into the clean echoing bowl that she clung to as if she might fall. He wrapped his arms around her shoulders and lowered her to lay on the floor.

"It can't hurt to rest your head on the cool tiles. I promise they're quite clean," he assured her. He gave her a few minutes and watched as she rolled part of her forehead on the floor as if taking his suggestion. When she began to moan and hugged herself tighter to hide her hand still in her purse, he spoke again. "I could fetch you something from the kitchen if you like, but it might do you some good to try to walk there with me."

Tanya kept her eyes mostly closed and nodded with a whine. She squished up her face as though she might cry and Solomon reacted as she had hoped by helping her to her feet and holding her close to him. She dragged her feet just enough to show she needed his help. She felt her cell phone vibrate next to her hand in her purse, swiped the screen, and held down the lower volume button.

Solomon gave her some reassuring words on the way to the kitchen. "You're gonna be just fine. Everybody overdoes it once in a while."

Once in the kitchen, Solomon helped guide her to a counter where she could lean and apologized for having no place to sit. He insisted on removing her purse and placed it on the counter in front of her with a grin. "Heavy little thing, isn't it? How long have you been carrying?"

Tanya almost gave away the game but pushed her hands up to her face and then guided some stray hairs behind her ears. She kept her eyes mostly lidded to feign sensitivity to the bright light as she looked back at him. "A girl can never be too careful, right? Do you have something bubbly to drink?"

"Of course, I almost forgot myself," Solomon answered. He produced a bottle of sparkling water and popped the top.

When he turned away from her to go to a door that must be his pantry, she took a quick look around. The light was bright, which was exaggerated slightly by the reflective surfaces. It reminded her of a restaurant kitchen for all its counter space and outlets for gadgets, but more spread out and clean than she was used to. It was a galley style kitchen with an island counter where a basic but unused-looking set of pots and pans and utensils hung organized from hooks overhead.

"This place is such a dream," Tanya said as she forced a smile. "I could see myself living in a place like this. It's like a little castle." She took a long drink from the bottle of bubbling water and covered her mouth just before a loud burp.

"Excuse me!"

"Please, pace yourself. Small swigs, until you're sure you can handle more," Solomon advised with a laugh. "Getting sick in here would not be pleasant to clean up." He returned to her side and placed a few napkins, a package of crackers, and a small sugar-coated fruit bar on the countertop. "The pâte bars always soothe my stomach, so I thought it might help. It's been a staple I can't seem to do without since my Legion days. I probably ought to at least learn your name before I go on too much about myself."

When the pâte was offered, Tanya hesitated at first, breaking the bar in half to look at the inside. The gooey jam bar gave a pleasant but muted berry aroma. She greedily took a bite with a nod of gratitude and responded to the taste with a tight-lipped moan. While still chewing, she admitted, "I don't eat many sweets. My cheeks are tingling. I'm sorry," she placed a hand over her mouth when she heard herself until she properly swallowed. "I swear, I do have some manners. I'm Tanya."

Solomon smiled broadly. "Take some time here to get your bearings, Tanya. My associate, Mr. Christian, will come to show you to a room for the night. I can't put you out and trust you'll get home safely in such a state. As you're my guest, my conscience won't allow it." He turned to leave while she finished her snack.

Tanya waited until she could no longer hear his footsteps and opened the pantry door to inspect its holdings. She took a handful more of the bars to tuck into her purse and noted that most of the contents were canned goods like salmon, soups, ready-to-eat meals, and some dry stock items like paper towels and trash bags in a hanging basket on the door.

She noted the hanging wine glasses under a cupboard near a block of kitchen knives when she heard returning steps and made her way to the sink to wash her hands with her back turned to the doorway. "Is there a towel in- Oh, god!" Tanya blurted when she turned to look at him. "I'm sorry. Are you okay?"

The man Solomon had been speaking to before held the wrist of his slung arm and gave her a nod. "Miss Tanya, was it?" he asked with a polite grumble. He had a small bandage above his left eye where his hair may have met if it hadn't receded into a horseshoe of dark brown carefully trimmed around his ears. He wore aviator-style glasses that appeared to have recently been bent and did not sit quite right on his taped nose. "I've had better days," he forced a wheezing laugh. "Mr. Solomon asked me to escort you to your room for the night when you're ready."

"How did it happen?" She asked as he pulled open the pantry to offer her a paper towel roll. She took it and dried her hands and then made a show of looking for a place to discard the used towels. "Was it that break-in earlier?"

He offered his hand to take them to a waste can under the sink and then returned with his hand out again. "A story for another time, perhaps. May I inspect your purse? Mr. Solomon informed me that you carry some protection. For our peace of mind, I would like to see that it's properly secure

84

while you are recovering. We don't want any accidents. I hope you understand."

Reluctantly, Tanya pointed to her purse on the counter. "I guess I have had too many drinks tonight. Better safe than sorry. Do you need to take it?"

"Oh, I'm not taking it from you," he replied. "Just going to make sure your actions are deliberate." He reached into the purse, placing the small handgun in his sling hand, checked the safety, removed the magazine, and pulled the slide to make sure the chamber was clear. After he replaced the pistol in her purse, he pulled one of the syringes from the pocket. He turned it over and put it back inside. When he heard Tanya about to protest he held up a hand. "Relax. It's a party. Some of our guests get carried away up here, and that's fine. If you share, be clear in what you have here. If it's for yourself, be aware that an ambulance takes almost twenty minutes to arrive once we've called them. I'm trained in basic first aid, but I assure you, it won't do much good if you overdo it. Are we clear?"

Tanya swallowed hard and gave him a tight-lipped nod. She picked up her purse and ate a cracker. "I kinda thought Riff would take me home. Is he too drunk to drive?"

"I haven't seen him," Mr. Christian answered quickly. "If I do, I'll point him in your direction to get you home. The others already left for the night so I assumed he did as well. Come on, let me show you upstairs so you can settle down and get some sleep. I'll fetch a bathrobe to hang outside your door if you'd like me to launder your clothes for tomorrow."

"I can just call a cab," Tanya suggested.

"I think you'd do better to accept Mr. Solomon's invitation to stay," he said with a tone of finality. "As the newest acquaintance, he informed me he has a day planned for you tomorrow to better get to know each other. As a budding young businesswoman, it may be a rare opportunity for you that you won't want to miss. And it may just be the only way to get an invitation to return for his next soirée." He waited a moment to gauge her hesitant reaction. "Mr. Solomon is likely to consider it very poor manners of you to run off in the middle of the night after he's asked you to stay."

"That's quite an offer," Tanya answered reluctantly. "I think I've got my feet back under me at least. Lead the way, Mr. Christian."

***

Melissa had spent much of the night skulking on the second-floor balcony. She waited quietly in a shadowy corner near the room she had chosen for her quarters and watched as the parlor doors remained closed. Just as she believed the events of the evening had passed, the familiar blonde woman emerged with an escort to a space out of sight beneath the grand stairway. Some time went by and the gentleman in a tuxedo returned to the parlor alone.

Mr. Solomon and his bodyguard returned to the main hall while discussing their new guests. Solomon mentioned her name with instructions of caution and Melissa made an effort to focus on his intentions. As she concentrated on what he might mean, their conversation broke and Solomon moved out of sight.

Mr. Christian looked up toward the balcony as if he knew he was being watched, though he didn't seem to know where from. He adjusted the jacket draped around his slung shoulder and made his way to the parlor to show their guests out and thank them for coming.

Once the rest of them had left the mansion, her attention was drawn back to the bottom of the stairs where Solomon helped the blonde woman walk through the main hall and under where Melissa stood. She couldn't see the woman's face as it was shrouded by her hair and the closeness to Solomon's chest.

Mr. Christian could be seen across the way, setting the parlor back in order. In the space of a blink, she rushed to the doorway of the room and surprised him as he was reducing the gas valve to the fireplace. She stepped behind the bar and poured the uncapped brandy into one snifter and then another.

"I suppose you're hoping for an apology for my actions earlier this evening?" While her hands remained hidden behind the bar, Melissa swiftly dug a fingernail into her wrist and added a trickle of her blood to one glass. "And I may have overreacted. But as I'm sure you're aware of my first meeting with Mr. Solomon and his friends, I may have given the impression that I'm willing to be used. I should have been more clear how I feel about separating work and play."

She swirled both glasses in her hands and approached the bodyguard who stood proudly as if the injuries against him were no bother. "I don't drink on the job. And I'm always on the job."

Melissa feigned a laugh and again reminded him of his transgression. "You don't go into business for yourself or get too handsy on the job either, right? And you never step out of line, or at least when your master is watching." She stepped closer until she had to look up at the man to meet his eyes and test his mettle to see if he would stand his ground. When he didn't move, she offered him the blood-tampered drink.

Reluctantly, Mr. Christian nodded. "One drink. No games. And a truce between us," he demanded. "I do you no harm, and you do me no harm."

"It couldn't be simpler," she smiled as he took the glass. She clinked her snifter against his, and Melissa waited for him to drink. Once he had done so, she took his glass and watched as his eyes rolled and his knees wobbled. "Aw, look at that. For such a big man, you might just be a lightweight drinker."

Mr. Christian steadied himself on the mantle and he looked wildly around the room as if he were suddenly shrouded in darkness. His horrified expression widened with eyes that turned to cracked silver. "What is this?"

"This," she said, setting the glasses on the bar without taking a drink from her own, "is my way of keeping the deal we've just made. You will continue to be in Mr. Solomon's service as usual. But as my blood courses through your veins, you will know me as your new mistress. Don't worry, I don't ask much. Just that if I call upon you, you will come. You will serve on my demand. And I will reward you with more of my special gift. How is your shoulder feeling?"

He made a fist and then straightened his arm out of the sling with a slight wince of pain. "I don't understand." He reached up and bent and squeezed his taped nose, then inhaled a deep breath through it.

"You'll keep up the charade of being hurt for now," Melissa went on. "After all, that injury is still fresh. But, as I understand, you have a fair amount of work to do securing the house as Mr. Solomon ordered."

"How did-"

"Hush now, I'm not finished." Melissa approached him again and lifted his chin with one upturned fingernail. "Now you'll be able to do your work, and each night, you may come to me to quench your thirst, so long as I am pleased by your performance. Your beast problem needs a swift solution. I cannot be called upon to keep fixing it. I'm certain Mr. Solomon would not want his new captives to come to any harm or be able to break free. So part of your security additions should include a vented vault. Or two, if you wish to keep them fed without tearing each other apart."

"They'd kill each other?" Mr. Christian asked.

Melissa stared into his eyes and removed her finger with a

sharp flick. "It's my belief that's what they were trying to do before they caught sight of your other guests. I couldn't have a blood bath ruin my stay here, could I? I also need you to come to the room I'll be staying in, on the east-facing corner upstairs, and properly mask that window before morning. And lastly," she added, "don't do anything to betray Mr. Solomon on my behalf unless I ask it of you. I can handle myself just fine. Do you understand?"

"Yes, mistress. I mean, Miss Johnston."

Melissa pinched his cheek. "Good boy. Now go."

Chapter Eleven - Another Door Closes

Before he could get the door open, the phone was ringing in the office at the garage. Blake grabbed the receiver and started to look around for a pen, "Good morning, Whiskey Throttle."

He found a pen but immediately tossed it onto the desk calendar and started to remove the costume jacket he used for cutting pre-recorded promotional segments for the underground wrestling company. It was decorated across the back, cuffs, and shoulders with shiny plastic studs and had silver sequins across the lapels that formed the letters J and R, respectively.

"What do you mean, tonight?" Blake argued into the phone. "You said I was suspended until Murphy- Yeah, I do vaguely remember you saying something about training. Is it another new kid? Hold on, I'm setting up the shop, let me put you on speaker."

He hung his jacket on a back wall hook and flipped on the desktop computer while the call continued with Stan's heavy huffs almost crackling in the speaker. "This guy is a veteran, I said! So you don't have to worry about carrying him. But he doesn't bump well. So I'm asking you to work with him and do a match or two to make him look like a monster to take on Murphy when he gets back."

"Hey, now we're talking," Blake answered as he noticed the

tone for call waiting and watched the red light blink on a second line. "I can do a squash, no problem. Unless you had something else in mind?" Blake flipped the OPEN sign into position on the door and sank deep into his chair to lean back.

Stan wheezed deeply and continued. "I'm gonna need you to get out there and run your mouth a few minutes. Whatever you gotta do to brag or play heel and get the crowd to absolutely hate you. Bring a bent chair if you need to remind them of the match. I'm gonna come out and try to put you in line, and you grab hold of me, and his music is gonna hit. Then you toss me or drop me, whatever you think, just call it so I can sell it. Then you're gonna walk into a springboard blockbuster. What do you think?"

"Stan, I think I'm working tonight," Blake grinned. "Do I need my gear for just one bump?"

"Wear whatever the hell you want. Maybe put some tape on your face from that headbutt or something though, huh?" Stan sounded like he was climbing stairs now, as out of breath as he was. "See ya around six for pre-show, alright kid?"

Stan ended the call and a red light flashed a waiting voicemail. Blake lit a cigarette and played the message as DX was coming through the door. The message was just the sound of an exasperated sigh and a beep to end the call.

DX placed a small bag on the desk. "One of your regular customers calling to compliment your work?"

Blake shook his head. "I doubt it. Whoever it was, we could use the work. What about you? You look like you got something on your mind."

DX poured a cup of coffee and laughed. "I hate to say you told me so, but that chick stood me up last night."

Blake flicked his ashes and leaned back in his chair. "How did I know it was a woman problem? I wouldn't worry about it too much. Like I said, she's just not easy to get close to."

"Well, how the hell do you know her then? I figured if she don't mind hanging around you, I'd be a trade-up." He took a long drink of the coffee and slouched in the chair across from Blake.

Blake pulled his hair tie out and re-tightened it in place. "If she and I had ever dated, you may have something there. But that never happened, and as long as I've known her, she hasn't really been on any dates. A buddy of mine has been climbing that tree for years and hasn't even reached a branch."

"It just doesn't add up. She asked me." DX finished his drink and tossed the cup into the waste can. "You got anything for us to work on today? I need something to shake it off. It shouldn't be a big deal, but as you can imagine, a guy like me doesn't just get brushed off like that."

Blake stood up and stubbed out his cigarette. "Can you work on cars?" he asked as he nodded to the parking lot where a full-sized sedan was coming into view.

"I can work on anything with an engine. I just want to be busy," DX admitted.

Blake made an irritated face and blew smoke from the corner of his mouth. "Get set up then, I'll go out and see what she wants."

The driver of the car wore large, dark sunglasses and had long, thick ginger hair. She opened the door of her midnight blue car and stepped out, looking up at Blake who had just closed the distance between them. She pulled up the strap of her heavy brown leather purse and put her hand out with a quivering smile. "Hi, I'm Joan. I called about my car a few days ago."

Blake looked down at the extended hand but didn't offer one back. "I know who you are. I got a guy in the garage ready to take a look if you'll go ahead and drive it in. I'll open the bay and you can wait in the office." He turned away from her almost as quickly as he approached. He re-entered the office and called out, "Open bay one."

When the car started again, they could hear a belt squealing and DX crossed his arms after pressing the wall button to raise the garage door. "Get ready to order a timing belt. Though a serpentine would mean more money."

Blake chuffed, "Whatever it is, estimate a replacement of everything you see that's even remotely worn or damaged."

DX shot him a confused look but nodded and turned back to wave the driver forward until the front bumper almost touched the back wall. Blake returned to the office and Joan followed after popping the hood.

She took off her purse to hang it over the chair back and raised her glasses into her hair. "I guess I deserve this cold shoulder you're giving me. That's why I figured giving you some business would buy me some time."

Blake closed the door to the garage just as DX was coming toward it. He put his hands up and turned back to the car to begin his inspection. Blake turned back and started in on her. "I don't care how or why you found me, but whatever your reason, I think you better get to it before I have a chance to open a thirty-year-old Pandora's Box of problems I have with you being here now."

Her lip trembled again. Her face showed lines of age, worry, and regret. Her eyes flashed anger and sadness mixing back and forth as she tried to find the right words. When they did come, she spoke slowly, as if speaking to a child. "Well, then without wasting any more time, I wanted to tell you my husband is dying. He was in a bad accident, several ribs were broken, and they found sources of internal bleeding. He's on life support but has water on the brain. And I know I shouldn't have taken so long to find either of you, but I promised him I would come look for Simon and our daughter, your sister Leila. That's when I promised myself I should find you, too."

Blake shook his head and set his jaw. "Simon, huh? I should have known it was something like that. If you wanted to find me at any point while living your new life, it shouldn't have

95

been too difficult."

Joan glared back at his accusing tone. "I am not here to apologize for leaving your father," she said after calming herself. "And I'm not here to get scolded for being a terrible mother either. I just needed to see you before you go to prison for twenty more years and I could talk to you without a pane of glass between us."

Joan reached into her purse for a picture frame and a pack of cigarettes and put them both on the desk while rifling through the bag for something else. Blake pulled a lighter from his desk drawer and set it next to the picture before turning it for a better look. The framed photo was that of Simon in his early teen years. Wedged into the corner, a wallet-sized school picture of Blake had begun to curl and crack where it stuck out from the frame. He was maybe twelve or thirteen then, with a thick, ginger bowl cut and his cheeks covered in freckles.

"How did you know about my trial?" Blake asked flatly as she lit a smoke and offered him one. He waved her away and pulled one of his own.

She took a long drag and crossed her legs as Blake pushed an ashtray to the center of the desk. "I briefly dated Jack Poffo, who is now the police chief. I've asked him several times to keep an eye on you after... After what happened to Mick. He had just made detective when you started working for Louis. Jack was in and out of trouble a lot before he became a cop, so I knew he could blend in with the kind of company you were keeping in that place. Even before it became a sleazy strip club."

"Gentleman's club," Blake corrected.

"Whatever you want to call it. You were in with the mob, then the couple of years you ran with those bikers." Joan looked at the garage door and grinned. "As if I wouldn't recognize Deacon after all these years. You two were so close when you were little boys, I'm not surprised to see him with you now. Where has he been?"

Blake pushed smoke in a heavy cloud from both nostrils. "He's not with me. Deac just works here for now. He'll be headed back to Arizona once I'm out from under these allegations. He came out to check on me. That's what family does." He crushed his cigarette out as if punctuating his accusing statement.

Joan nodded with a look of defeat. "I'm not saying I don't deserve it, but it would mean a lot to me if you could cut me some slack. If I thought you would have come with me after they killed your father, I would have come for you. I couldn't stand the sight of their goddamn suits and hear the way they manipulated this city with their smooth words and buying off cops like they were above the law."

Blake pushed his lips together until he could feel his mustache stubble tickle his nose. "They didn't kill Mickey. They should have. And they came to kill him. But I think you ought to know that if anyone in that piece of history gets your disapproval, you ought to know that I did it. Those men threw him in front of me and gave me the chance to right everything wrong in my life, and I took it. I earned that moment that no one could be allowed to take from me. I did it for us. And then it was just me anyway."

Joan's face flushed bright red and her mouth moved wordlessly as she searched Blake for any shred of emotion. "Oh, my God!" she whispered.

They both sat in silence until her cigarette burned down to her shaking knuckles. She blinked like she was seeing Blake for the first time as an entirely different person and let her tears streak down her face. Joan sat forward to toss the butt in the ashtray and pulled out another cigarette. When she fumbled with the lighter, Blake stood to put his hand over hers and lit it for her.

Joan held him there a moment and kissed his hand. "If there's anything I can do-"

"You can." he stopped her. "You can walk out that door, and go be with your husband. He needs you. My breakfast is getting cold. I like to eat while my hands are still clean." He pulled away as she was still reaching for him and went to the closet bathroom and pulled the door shut. Blake heard something hit the floor in the office as he turned on the faucet to wash his hands and face. Then he heard the squeal of the damaged belt in Joan's car before he came out while drying his hands.

DX stood in the office looking down at the broken picture frame on the paint-chipped concrete floor. "I thought I recognized her. You good, brother?"

"It's not my worst day. Not my best," Blake replied. "I'll clean this up. I'm thinking of closing for the day. Gotta get prepped for my other job tonight anyway. Are you doing anything later?"

"Hey man, whatever you got, I'm in." DX went into the garage to close the bay door and brought back a broom.

***

A pulsing darkness slowly filled the horizon and beat down from a celestial halo of surrounding, growing, eclipsed suns that shimmered and cracked as they invaded each other's corona. The weight of their heat pressed from inside her body outward while every extremity pricked with acute, splitting pain. The sensation of flayed flesh was somewhat a consolation against a landscape of bubbling, boiling sand that popped ribbons of green fire below.

Brimstone and patchouli swirled between divergent paths ahead that battled each other to be traversed. The green fire spread and began to crest in parting seas to reveal the carefully crafted stones within each path before flinging themselves away from immense wells of reaching hands. Their skin crawled with vermin that burrowed inward until the outer layer melted away to the bones made of briar vines.

The suns launched forward and ripped the velvet sky apart with explosions of drakes and gargoyles and krakens that shrieked in distant echoes before they swarmed each other. A water well reached up in molten sinewy fingers to pull until the maw closed above in a thundering cascade of collapsing overture.

The well-throat crumbled down into caressing whispers. The gentle reminders became searing droplets of freezing time, trickle-ticking faster along body limbs before they broke and grew into mirrored splashes. These jagged and mercurial kaleidoscope fractals spun and swam through each other and bent blinding light from an unseen source to reveal faces in various states of grief.

The images were familiar for only a moment before they challenged each other for attention. Then they consumed each other and the faces within them shattered with screams of the most familiar voices, all in her names.

"Rose."

"Little Flower…"

"Melissa."

"Miss Johnston?"

"MISSY!"

Her mouth opened to speak but her tongue flew away as one bestial hand clapped around her throat and another spitted her body from bottom to top to hang, endlessly rotating, forced to watch her heart drip toward her lips. A force unseen pinned her arms to keep them from reaching as her mind screamed for the image most familiar. "TILLY!"

Chapter Twelve - Stirring Echo Chamber

Simon turned the corner from the alley just as Blake was locking the door at the garage office. He ran the length of the parking lot on all fours and changed just as Blake turned around. Simon grabbed him by the collar and slammed him against the glass and glowered.

"Who is in that house?" Simon barked. His eyes moved wildly back and forth between Blake's as they searched for answers before the man could speak.

Blake's hands gripped Simon's wrists and tried to push back as his feet left the ground. "Get your goddamn hands off me! What house?"

Simon seethed and threw his brother across the pavement where he rolled to a stop on one knee. Blake stood quickly but Simon had already advanced and took hold of him by the throat and demanded, "You told me it was safe. That it was empty. You set a fucking trap and I want to know why!"

Another man close to Simon's size rounded the building wearing riding leathers, gloves, and a red helmet with a tinted, closed visor. In one of his hands was a spiked knuckle knife and with the other he removed his helmet and held the strap ready to swing with it.

"I think you're picking a fight with the wrong guy, cabrón!" the man threatened. "Maybe you want to see how well you handle two-on-one?"

When Simon turned to address the new man, Blake lifted his knee into his brother's belly and threw an elbow into his jaw. Simon's eyes flashed a bright yellow and he growled while rolling his head across the back of his neck and then again to center. He tightened the grip on Blake's throat as he pulled him closer. Blake's face swelled and reddened as he tried to show no fear while struggling to breathe.

"You ought to know better than that. I'm not some idiot drunk at your little club you can work over," Simon warned through clenched teeth.

Simon felt a blade sink into his back and turned just in time for the helmet to strike him across the face. When his body turned, the biker's grip twisted with the knife which forced him to let go. Simon reached back to pull the knife out and cussed in agony as he flung it away behind him, then just as easily took hold of the biker with both hands by his jacket breast and threw him into the motorcycle parked near the bay door.

Blake tackled Simon to the ground and was flipped over onto his back. Simon stood over him, blocking the sun, and then stepped on his chest, digging his heel in and pressing him down. "You can't win this fight. Tell me what I want to know."

Blake grabbed at Simon's ankle and tried to lift it. "I've never backed down from a fight," he wheezed. "And I would never-"

"Never what? Set me up?" Simon accused as his brow bled down his cheek. "Like the way you set up Tanya to be bait for your sister?"

"MY sister? Do you mean the sister YOU watched over for all those years and then let slip through your fingers? Man, that's rich. And Tanya, huh? Fuck you! YOU told me to get rid of one of those girls, while YOU went soft on the other and got too close! Save one and sacrifice many." Blake reminded him between grunts as he kept pushing and pulling to get free. "Just another time I had to clean up after you! I had to get my business up and running again afterward without your help so the others didn't know what went down in that VIP room. Left with no other choice than to burn your leftovers on the roof. Then I had to figure out how to give my dancers and the bouncers back the means to feed themselves. But that was all for nothing, wasn't it?"

Simon's hair fell forward creating a shroud of shadow over his face that hid his expression.

Blake's face was turning color again from his struggle but he refused to give up. "And NOT ONCE did you admit fault in any of that shit show that happened to ANY of my crew or my girls that were burned alive because of YOUR precious pack! Don't think I'll ever forget your Thanksgiving where I had to sit there and watch as you let that murderer back in after he torched our place to the ground. And I was right there left hung out to dry when YOU couldn't handle the fight YOU couldn't win without MY help. And how many died while you were handling things? Why am I supposed to look at a monster and see the good in him but you can't?"

When Simon let up the pressure Blake pushed his foot away and got himself back onto his knees. The other biker had recovered and was charging when Blake shook his head and put up his hand. "Deac, stop! It's over. Either way, if he wants to finish it, just let it be."

Deacon held his ground and shot looks between both men. "He wrecked my bike, bro. Anything else, but nobody wrecks my bike!"

"Yeah, yeah. I know," Blake waved before he spat on the ground. "And I'll settle that if I make it through today. But just let this one go. For me."

Deacon cracked his neck and punched the bay door. "So what is all this? Some old score need settled, or what?"

"It's none of your business," Simon said quietly.

"You gonna just roll up in here and throw- How did you throw me like that anyway?" Deacon shook his head and refocused. "And throw me over there and put hands on mi hermano and then tell me it's none of my business? What? How are you even breathing? I gutted you on the spot and you bleeding all down your back. I ain't cleaning that up, by the way," he informed Blake.

"And Tanya? Like, little blondie Tanya?" Deacon looked to Blake, who shrugged and nodded. "Man, you just wrapped up in everybody's life! And now you just standing there all bloody and unbothered like nothing happened, like you didn't just start a bunch-a shit, not knowing just how much it IS my business and try telling me to step off?"

Blake stood and rolled his shoulders and stretched his back. "This is the last time you come to where I eat, make a big mess, and run off with your tail wagging like you're the only one who gives a damn about anybody or anything. How about you actually handle some of your own business for a change and go talk to your father before he dies? Isn't that why you started bugging me in the first place? To be the hero and make Daddy proud? How's that working out for ya?"

Simon stared at his reflection in the office window and placed both hands and his forehead on the cold glass to lean as Deacon pulled a smashed pack of cigarettes from his pocket and offered one of the unbroken ones to Blake.

"Joan just left," Blake continued, putting on his gloves and zipping his sequin costume jacket. "She tracked me down because she thought I could find you for her. Ain't that a kick in the pants? I sure as hell ain't going to go pay my last respects to some old man who kept letting his problems fall into my lap. He's laid up at Gia's hospital. I got shit to do."

The sound of sirens in the distance snapped Simon back to the moment. He changed form in front of the other men and ran between them toward the alley on his way back out of the city.

***

The echoing murmur didn't stop even after Tanya woke up tangled in the satin sheet and cashmere blanket in the four-post bed of Mr. Solomon's guest bedroom. The room was mostly bare but for the protruding silvery paper fan border around the carefully spaced rectangular sections of the mauve walls. An open, charcoal-colored woodgrain door led to a personal bathroom, and another smaller set of double doors that were closed led to a walk-in closet, with a third to match that would take her back to the main hall balcony.

She held her head as it throbbed her pulse back into her hands while the sound of a woman's voice kept calling to her. She searched her purse for a tiny bottle of pills but found it to be empty. She tossed the bottle back inside and grabbed her phone only to find it wouldn't turn on except for a flash of a red lightning bolt before the screen blinked out.

"Oh, come on! You can't be serious!" she huffed. "I'm just batting a thousand this week."

The sound of a big rig brake pressure release outside the window was followed by the beeping alert of the truck backing up toward the mansion. When she went to look, she could see Mr. Christian going to speak to the truck driver and sign papers on a clipboard. His arm was no longer in a sling, and though there were tree branches and some distance between them, she couldn't see any bandage on his face where it had been the night before.

The rig held only one large, cube-shaped object like a drab, sturdy storage shed. When the beeping stopped, the driver jumped out of the cab and got to work pulling straps and setting heavy braces into place to safely move the structure.

Tanya could hear the spectral, wispy voice again like it was right behind her, maybe even in the room with her. The word repeating and the voice speaking became a little clearer as she moved closer to the bedroom door. She squished her face in subtle pain and concentration and found herself out of breath when she recognized the voice.

"I'm trying, Missy. I'm trying," Tanya shook her head with her eyes squeezed tightly shut. "But you gotta let me think."

She went back to the bed to pick up her purse and made her way out to the balcony facing the main hall. On the back of the door, as promised, a thick terry cloth robe hung with a small tote bag and she squeezed and rubbed the material against her cheek while considering changing out of her clothes. She put it on over her outfit for an added layer of warmth and turned to go downstairs toward the kitchen. The patio glass that was broken last night was now covered in thick weather-tight plastic with a matching zipper doorway. Just outside this layer was where the storage structure was being lowered off the truck. She hurried along to avoid any attention from Mr. Christian and, once in the kitchen, began searching the kitchen drawers for any kind of pain relief pills.

When she couldn't find anything helpful, she opened the refrigerator for a bottle of water and unwrapped another fruit bar from those she had stashed in her purse. Tanya left the kitchen to explore the ground floor while keeping a lookout for either of the men. She made her way around the main hall and couldn't help but notice the contours of the high ceiling. The intricate trimmings and murals were hidden mostly in shadows despite the rays of natural light from the large bay windows while the grand chandelier was unlit.

She brought her attention back down to a door she found to be locked, then saw another to hurry to, only to find it locked as well. Each of them bore hand-carved reliefs but she kept herself moving rather than linger on the details.

A muted banging, followed by a warbled howling sound made her turn toward the stairs where she saw Mr. Solomon closing a door on the balcony above and turning a key to lock it. She ducked into the parlor which was still open, and turned to watch once she was behind the bar. He had reached the bottom by the time she was in place, and she could see the sleeves on his crisp, white shirt were rolled up to the elbow and his hair was wet and combed back like he had just showered. He walked with a determined pace to the plastic zipper door to meet Mr. Christian outside and oversee the last moments of the structure delivery.

She made her way to the window to see the opposite vantage point that her bedroom had offered. From here, she could see down into the parking lot where Riff's car was still parked. Beyond the lot were low, rolling hills and sweeping fairways of the seasonally closed golf course. There were some barren trees that split part of the course and a pond reflecting the mostly cloudy sky above.

Tanya took a step backward into someone who grabbed her arms firmly just above the elbow.

"Curiosity killed the cat," came Solomon's delighted voice.

She took a breath and relaxed in his grip. "Maybe it was too content to stay away." Tanya turned to face him.

Solomon gave a toothy smile. "Close enough, I suppose. Does that mean you've found something to satisfy your curiosity?"

Tanya hesitated and closed her robe with crossed arms as she made some space between herself and her host. "This place. It's just not quite like the mansion of my dreams. Don't get me wrong. The decor is fabulous. I'm guessing it's restored to its original, or very well-imitated, 19th century? The reliefs on interior walls and ceilings, the carved doors, the skeleton key locks, big amazing rooms to entertain guests, and, of course, the crystal chandelier! But the little girl in me hoped for a library with rolling ladders, suits of armor, hand-painted portraits, and secret rooms hidden behind trick walls."

Solomon's eyebrows pushed together more seriously and his smile closed but remained. "Well, I'd hate to disappoint you, and I will admit that I'm a bit of a show-off. But some of those things might not quite meet your dreams. For instance, I have a library, or rather, a massive room with shelves. But what books I have are still yet to be unpacked. That room is locked off until I can clean and restore it, and hopefully refill the shelves. I do have one or two pieces of armor, but they're modern, practical pieces made of kevlar. However, if you follow me, I do actually have two such trick doors that I'd be more than happy to show you."

When he offered his hand, Tanya took it and walked with him back into the main hall and to a wall panel near where

Lanny had escorted her to the under-stair bathroom the night before.

"It's not exactly a secret, but this room has the spacing I desired and none of the elaborate wall trimmings to be concerned about damaging."

Solomon pressed against a piece of trim that appeared to be added in as an afterthought and a large section of the wall swung inward to reveal a room whose lights flickered on as he and Tanya entered. Once inside, she could see glass-cased cabinets along the walls that were filled with a variety of weapons. Just inside the door on one side was a series of fencing swords in a fanned rack with their blades crossed at the bottom. An obi belt was folded beneath a polished daisho, and above it was a musket and flintlock pistol. Between cabinets, with space to spare, was a small bench that was carved into wood and painted to look like a human on their hands and knees.

Before she could take a closer look at the entire collection, Tanya asked, "Are all of these real?"

"You can hold them and use them if that's what you mean. I've bought them from museum displays and auctions," Solomon explained. "But many of them are replicas and knock-offs. I like the history, even if I've never cared about authenticity. Besides, many of these, if they were historical artifacts, would be quite impossible to purchase. But I've kept what appeals to me and have spent some time with many of their modern equivalents to improve my understanding of their practical uses."

"Oh, so you're not just some history professor who hunts relics like in the movies," Tanya joked. "Then you must be a soldier, maybe a Marine?"

"Something like that. But that's all in the past, I'm afraid," he answered quickly. "Old habits are hard to break. Like stale-tasting fruit bars and not feeling comfortable in a bed. A place like this should make it easy to forget trenches and fox holes and shells blasting so close that the soldier next to you is taken while you hold for orders." He paced around an empty podium in the center of the room, dragging his fingers along the wood grain of its elevated base. "But that's just not the case. My oven timer sounds like an IED. Sometimes the way door latches click into place reminds me of a bullet chambering. Even the golf course outside, which I thought would let me see so far away that I'd know there's nothing to fear, sometimes reminds me of No Man's Land, and the shadows and hidden spaces on the rolling fairways can just as easily take me back to feeling like I'm being watched by a patient sniper."

Tanya watched his expression as if it would change as he spoke, but he held a gentle, almost apologetic smile. "So then why stay? There must be somewhere that suits your needs, even if you can't throw your parties or take your collections."

Solomon lowered his chin and broke eye contact with a gentle nod. "I don't want to speak out of place," he said as he stepped closer and took her hands. He waited until their eyes met again to go on quietly. "But as a beautiful young woman living in a sprawling city, surely you must also sometimes feel like no place will ever truly feel safe. Like that streetlight doesn't ever provide quite enough light. Or the pedestrian you stopped for, because you're supposed to, could just stop in front of your car and decide your kindness should be repaid with malice. But you don't lock your door because he might hear it click, and you'd feel guilty for insulting him if he's just an innocent like you, going about your day."

Tanya couldn't help but cry. She steeled her jaw, drew her lips to a stiff, straight line, and nodded with him as the first tear touched the corner of her mouth. "Why would you ever let some stranger into your home, then? Let them drink your champagne and sleep in your bed, and," she laughed with a sniff, "and wear your clothes?"

He let go of her hands and watched as she dried her eyes. "Because when you live with fear, and train with fear, and fight with fear for so long, you have to learn to make fear your ally instead of your enemy. Because I refuse to be prey to the monster that makes my skin crawl. When it makes my spine tingle, or my nose itch, or that inexplicable cold feeling, I can feel him warning me. He's telling me to prepare. To respond. To not be a victim. And something tells me, you are the kind of woman who feels the same way."

"You sound like my father. The way he would sit down to talk to Melissa and me while we were having an ice cream on a sunny day in the park. He, uh," her lip shook violently, preventing her words from coming. She tried to gesture with her hands as if she were still speaking, but when her words wouldn't come out she covered her mouth and her heated, embarrassed cheeks. She held her hands there over her face and heard the echoing voice of her sister again as if she were answering the mention of her name.

"It sounds like your father is a wise man. It seems a shame to ruin such a sweet moment in the sun, but he saw you at your most vulnerable. Your most innocent. With the least amount of fear in your heart while he could protect you." His tone had changed to something more threatening. Something almost angry. "And where is your sister now, miss, uh, Tanya…I just realized I don't even know your full name. My list of bad host etiquette needs to be trimmed." He extended his hand as if he were meeting her for the first time.

Tanya saw his extended hand through her fingers, lowered her guard to shake it, and laughed sheepishly. "It's Johnston. Tanya Johnston. I'm honored to be invited to this tour of your breathtaking home." She saw his face was gravely serious as they shook hands. His grip was overly strong, and she had to make a conscious effort to keep smiling.

"Your dream isn't over, Miss Johnston." He stared fiercely into her eyes and finally let go of her hand. "This house has a few more secrets I'd like you to see. I'll give you some time to wash up first. Your makeup is running, and I need to make a quick phone call and check on Mr. Christian's progress. Would you meet me in the parlor? Help yourself to a drink if you like."

Solomon left the room and Tanya with her arms out at her sides. She scolded herself. "That's what you do, T. Just start to get close to somebody and scare him off by getting too personal too fast." She left the armory room and pulled her robe tighter against a chill, then made her way to the parlor.

She turned the key on the fireplace to help get warm and went to the bar to decide if it was too early for a drink.

Chapter Thirteen - Accept No Substitution

Blake waved Deacon to pull over at Second Skin when he saw an older woman speaking with some police in front of a broken window. The woman was holding a broom and was quite animated as she answered their questions.

Once parked, Deacon dismounted and took another look at the scratched paint and broken mirror on his bike. "Man, who was that dude? You ain't said nothing since we split-"

"I said I'd settle it. Looks like we're not the only ones having problems today." Blake took off his helmet and hung it on the handlebars. He approached the same officer who came to his garage to harass him. "Sergeant Gordy, I hate to interrupt. I left a message before leaving the shop to say I was closing early today."

"This doesn't concern you, Gentry. Move along," Gordy replied. "Nice jacket. Are you trying to impress your new boyfriend here?"

Blake ignored the insult. "I just wanted to check in on my friend who runs the shop. Is she okay?"

Gordy turned to tell his partner he'd be right back. "If you know anything about the owner, maybe you could tell us when you last saw her. A Miss Tanya Johnston? Her employee says she hasn't answered her phone all morning and then found the window broken and possible signs of a struggle inside."

Blake nodded, "Uh, yeah, she had her car at my shop this week. We normally just do bikes, but a favor for a friend never hurts your karma, right?"

"Not really in your interest to be doing work for free after I reminded you of your fines being due," Gordy smirked and leaned back on his heels. "It also makes you a suspect, declaring she might owe you something. Not very smart." Gordy was holding a small notepad and turned a page to start writing.

"Transparency, right? I thought you guys preferred full disclosure," Blake quipped back. "No sense getting caught in a lie later. But to be clear, she's not in debt to me. Maybe she took out a loan? These main street shops aren't cheap."

"You ought to know about loans. Are you telling me I ought to go have a chat with Mr. Carelli? Are you still working for him?" Sgt. Gordy asked.

"I guess I walked into that, huh? As I've said many times, I no longer have any ties to Louis Carelli. Tanya is a good girl, she'd go for a legit bank loan," Blake huffed. "I should probably go, I'm almost out of trip time on the monitor. I was asked to cover at my second job tonight. Do you want me to call in again to make it official, or is telling you now good enough?"

"Do it right, Gentry. Call my desk, and leave a message. I can be pretty forgetful when I'm out doing real police work and not just checking on flight risks like you." Gordy gestured with his pen. "How did you get that busted honker anyway?"

Blake returned to his motorcycle and pulled on his helmet with the visor open. "Work accident. Come down and see for yourself tonight if you like. Who knows what'll happen at this show? If you don't have the address, just follow my tracker."

"You mean that fake sissy stuff you call 'rasslin' where you roll around with men in their underpants? Hard pass. If your friend turns up, call it in. For all we know, she did this herself for the insurance money."

Blake punctuated the officer's last word with a loud rev of his engine and walked the bike back to point toward the street. He flipped the visor down and took off toward his apartment.

When they arrived at a simple, multi-level brick building, Deacon started in again. When he drew breath to speak, Blake shot him a look. "Alright, I'm not gonna mention the bike again. But I want to know how long you've known about that guy in the parking lot."

Blake hung his helmet inside the door and checked his bag of ring gear. "Simon and I go way back. I've known him almost as long as you."

Deacon waited until Blake stopped to give him his full attention. "You know what I mean. The yellow eyes, the strength, the fur. I nearly shit myself and you're just taking

117

swings at this dude when you knew he was- I'm just gonna say it. He's a wolf-man."

Blake didn't stop undressing, hanging his riding leathers over a chair back and placing all his things near the duffel bag that held his ring gear for his appearance later. "He is," Blake shrugged with wide open arms. "There's no other way to say it, Deac. I can't sugar-coat it. I can't deny it. But at least you believe what you saw. I don't have to convince you that some geek off the street can just roll up and manhandle a couple of guys like us then walk off a stab in the back."

Deacon turned the chair toward him and sat on it backward, resting his arms over the back. "Alright, I need to level with you, 'cause I didn't think you would believe me until today. Remember I said I was gonna check in with my table? Yeah, well, there ain't anybody there to call. I put out a shout to a chapter closer to here. But Arizona? They're done." Deacon let his words linger a moment while he collected himself to try and keep his composure. "I saw the black dog on the highway. You know the stories truckers tell all the time? It ain't just some urban legend. And at the time, I thought I imagined the rest after our crew wrecked our bikes on I-10. Nothing to see for miles but hills and road markers. When I first saw something, I thought I was just tired. Except I was riding in the back of the pack and saw the shadows on either side of the road. Next thing I knew, we were all laid out."

Blake put a pot of water on the stove and pulled some hot dogs from the fridge along with some condiment bottles. "Keep talking, I'm listening."

118

"No, you're not, bro!" Deacon stood up and almost knocked the chair over. "I got slammed by something big and it knocked me out. When I came to, it was morning and the bikes were all still lying down, and the whole club was ripped and shredded, laying there for the vultures. There was so much blood on the highway. A trucker stopped and must have called it in. I think he was trying to ask me what happened when he was on the phone with the police. I went around and checked the boys, took their burner phones and wallets, and picked up my bike to head this way. All their shit is still in my saddle bag, and that old pal of yours knocked off the same mirror I had to fix on my way out here. I spent some of the money to have the scratches buffed out and some warmer clothes while trying to decide where to go."

Blake slit the package and dropped the hot dogs in and left the water boiling while he turned to address Deacon. He scratched at his neck with his knuckles and made sure his friend could see he wasn't ignoring him. "So you came here for what? You hoped I'd tell you that werewolves and boogeymen aren't real, and then I'd just go back to the desert with you to rebuild the Regulators from scratch? Only to find the first thing we'd have to tackle is more law snooping around for the sole survivor to lock up, and the guy who shares a juvie record with him for good measure?"

Deacon impatiently rolled his neck and balled his fists. "I don't think you're getting what I'm saying here."

"No, I get it," he answered quickly before he turned to lower the heat on the burner. He pulled a loaf of bread and counted out eight slices to stack between two plastic plates.

119

"I've seen some things myself. It takes a while to get used to it. If you ever do, that is. Believe it or not, Simon, Tanya, and I have gone hunting for things like that. It gets in you. You can't ignore it. It becomes an obsession, even when there's no real goal or purpose to it. It wrecks your life, costs jobs, and friends, and often you come up empty-handed, or stumble upon some muggers who wear funny masks and you gotta decide whether to do them in or turn them over. Not much of a choice when cops don't take too kindly to vigilantes."

Deacon had been pacing in what little space there was in the kitchen. He scratched his throat and his eyes flicked around the apartment like he was looking for something to break.

"Hey, will you stop a minute?" Blake shook up the condiment bottles, dressed his stack of bread, then used a fork from his dish rack to spear some over-cooked hot dogs out of the steaming water. "Sit down and breathe. I know it's not the best, but you need to eat too. It's a few hours yet until the show, then you can get yourself a couple of beers and order what you like there." He ate a few bites and waited for Deacon to get his plate. "It's not just nothing to me. It's some seriously twisted shit out there. I guess I'm just kinda numb to it in a way. And I'm in no position to go tearing off to settle a score in Arizona outnumbered. Speaking of riding, I'm gonna need to layer up if you insist on riding together in the worst part of winter because of your pride or whatever. Cars are warm and taxi services are plentiful. And that little costume jacket wasn't helping at all."

"And I can't hop in a cab and take off if trouble pops up. You do what you want." DX took a few minutes to eat quietly while mulling over their conversation. "So the guy that just kicked our asses, and the chick that stood me up, and YOU are some kind of nightmare hunter team?" He scrunched up his face like he was learning a new language. "Then he attacks you. The girl's shop is a mess and now she's MIA. Where does that leave you? Ain't you worried there's a bullseye on your back?"

Blake finished his lunch and tossed the plate in the sink. "I dunno. Maybe? But I got you to watch it now, right?" Blake winked and forced a laugh. "You went all-in for me today, which I appreciate, by the way. And I know my days are probably numbered. Hell, my knees aren't really up for it anymore. But until I can't do it, a lot of the time it's just hard not to. Sometimes I can't sleep, can't work, can't handle my business. I feel the hair on my neck stand up and gotta go see what's causing it."

Deacon showed his disdain for his friend's answer and matched Blake's throw to the sink with his plate. While still chewing a mouthful, he sputtered, "Oh, is that all, pendejo? Out of the frying pan, and into Infierno. For a second there, I thought you were gonna tell me some bad news."

Chapter Fourteen- Dangerous Liaisons

When Simon returned to the edge of the woods, Fisher met him with a disappointed look. "I don't know what you found out, but I don't want to believe that your brother has anything to do with it."

Simon shook his head and blew out a long breath. "Whether he does or not isn't important right now. For what it's worth, I don't believe it either. He's slippery and tries to misdirect when he lies. Today, he fought me." Simon turned to show the blood stain down his back.

"I saw," Fisher confirmed. "He pulled a knife on you? Doesn't that mean-"

Simon put a hand up, with his eyes drawn back to the hilltop mansion edging the golf course. "He had help. But he waved off his buddy like it should be fair. And Blake doesn't fight fair. He's either in too deep to ask for help or thinks I am." Simon looked over and grabbed the lapel of Blake's leather jacket that Fisher still wore until they were both behind a thick tree to keep out of sight. "Is there any reason we shouldn't get inside this place right now for Sam and Reno?"

"Yeah, there is. A couple of them," Fisher nodded. "Mama told me not to move until she comes back. And after a diesel truck came to drop off that shed," he pointed, "I lost her scent and I think she may be inside the house. It took an hour or more making a careful drop right in front of that broken window, so I figure it's some kind of heavy-duty vault."

"You said a couple? What else?"

Fisher avoided Simon's gaze as he looked down and ran his fingers through his hair. "I think the reason she is still in there is because they installed cameras all over the place. If we get close, they'll see. Which probably won't be a problem since, well, we're us," he chuckled when he looked back up. His smile faded quickly when Simon didn't join him. "But I checked out that last car in the lot. Somebody didn't leave the party last night. And I know it could be anybody, but it's not. The interior of the car had strands of blonde hair in the passenger seat and it smelled of booze and perfume. Uh, Tanya's perfume."

Simon shook his head as Fisher pulled a few strands of hair from his inside jacket pocket. Simon took them and pressed them under his nose to inhale deeply. "What the hell does that mean?"

A sound from behind Simon made him turn and they could see their companion, Mama, just as she returned to human form and tucked herself behind the same tree. She pulled both men down to crouch there with her.

"Keep your damn voices down," she whispered in warning. Mama traded scathing gazes with both men until she was sure she had their attention. "It means that girl done got caught up in our problems again. Now, we don't know what she doing here. But whatever it is, Mama don't want no angel blood on her hands, you hear?"

Simon hung his head. "You saw her?"

"Yeah, baby. I saw her through a window." Mama confirmed. "That hanging plastic is an easy way in, for now. But I was more concerned about gettin' out. So I didn't push it." Mama took a look around the trunk toward the house. "What about our Mr. Joshua? He showed us another way. Maybe we can find them and pull them over with us to that place?"

Simon stood and paced away from the mansion and then back. "And Tanya?"

Fisher met his gaze and boldly stated, "We have to put the pack first. You know as well as anyone that they aren't coming for us if we need it."

Simon clenched his teeth as Mama rose next to Fisher.

"I know she's special, baby. But Fisher's right," Mama agreed. "Once we have ourselves back together, we'll be stronger. Besides, we don't know what they're going through. If it were me or you in there instead, what would you want Reno to do?" Mama watched Simon closely as he weighed their words. "That's our family, baby. The one you started."

"The one we started, Phie."

Mama's eyes were wet as she squeezed them shut and pulled both men to her. She kissed each of their cheeks. "That's my boys," she winked at Fisher. "Come on, now. This damn cold about got Mama's tears freezing."

***

Solomon returned to find Tanya in the parlor finishing a glass of cranberry juice. "I apologize for the interruption. It's a busy day getting things back in order."

Tanya left the empty glass on the bar and met him with a smile. "For a moment there, I thought I said something wrong. Maybe I should get a cab out of here and get out of your way?"

Solomon remained serious and squeezed one of her hands and rubbed his thumb over her knuckles. "Oh, there's no need to waste a good day over my bad manners. I felt you could use a moment of privacy, and you reminded me I hadn't made a proper plan to have a guest for supper. I hope you won't mind that I've taken the liberty to choose for us. You will stay, of course?"

Tanya looked down at the strong hand holding hers and began to search for a way to politely refuse his offer.

"I insist. And then I'll do better than hire some strange driver to take you," Solomon pressed with a leaning grin. "I promised this place has a few more secrets for you. Please, let me show you one I've been keeping for some time."

Tanya returned a squeeze and followed as they crossed the main hall to one of the locked doors she encountered earlier.

Solomon reached into his pocket and showed her an old

brass skeleton key that was heavily tarnished with a very simple oval-ringed head. "I prefer to keep a few rooms locked for just such an occasion. It deters my party guests from wandering too far. And I'm quite fond of this old key. It's basic but sturdy and versatile. This key can access nearly any door in the house, which reminds me that the quality of several spaces has remained intact without the need for too many updates." he said as he pushed the door in to reveal a studio room.

A pair of large easels were turned on their side under a wrinkled tablecloth. Colorless lines of peeling paint edges showed on one wall where shelving had been removed. A tall arched window fed sunlight into the room over a dingy hardwood floor. An unlit brass-fixed pendulum light hung high with its adjustable chain wrapped tightly out of reach. A modern steel ladder leaned against an empty, sturdy bookshelf in the corner nearest the door, and a slim lectern stood in the corner farthest. Other shapes were arranged together neatly to one side, also covered in draped cloths. One may have been a bust or candelabra, another was broad and low like a lounge chair, and several squared edges may have been frames of canvases.

"Are you a painter, Mr. Solomon?"

"Adam, if you will," he insisted. "Well, not yet. It's an interesting idea to take up a new hobby. These things were left here when I moved in, and I just haven't decided what to do with the space. I was inspired by seeing these things, but lack the motivation to put them to use. But this is what I wanted you to see."

He took hold of the center shelf of the bookcase and pulled it to one side with a protest of aged squealing wheels. Solomon reached inside to press a clicking light switch. A series of bare-bulb lights showed stone stairs leading downward in a broad spiral into a cellar lined with brick. Tanya gave Solomon an eager look and he nodded toward the opening.

She took to the stairs without waiting and, only after a few steps, stopped to make sure he was following. She pulled her robe around her tightly and blew excited plumes of steaming breath as she made her way down. The brick outline stopped where the steps became a flat hard stone floor. The ceiling and walls were a room of smoother stone with some small but deep impressions that showed age and damage in different places. To either side, she could see the walls held racks made for bottles with many of the diamond-shaped openings still holding one in their space, but other sections were in various stages of age or disrepair. Centered on the floor was a large painter's drop cloth over a pair of parallel tracks that led toward a lumber-framed wall on the far side that was filled in with wooden planks and a large, thick, simple plank door with a basic metal bar latch like a backyard fence. Several modern totes lined a nearby wall that were filled with jars and bottles.

Tanya's excitement drained from her face as she scrunched her nose and covered her mouth with one arm. "The smell down here is so strong." She coughed into the crook of her elbow and turned to face her host. "Did something die down here?"

"That's quite a story I'm happy to tell, but it's not mine,"

Solomon answered as a half smile curled on his lips. "I should have warned you, but it would have spoiled the surprise. This room has been emptied of most of its contents. Barrels, bottles, jars, and most likely stills or mash tuns for crafting a variety of booze in the early 1900's. You're familiar with Prohibition, of course?"

"Oh yeah! It's only one of the most interesting pieces of American history," Tanya answered as she lowered her arm from her face. "I mean, even kids today have likely seen a movie or heard a history class story about Al Capone. But if I recall, they never could get him for hustling swill. It was his taxes or bookkeeping that caught up with him, which I can totally relate to. Numbers are not my strong suit."

"You're an intelligent young lady!" Solomon's impressed smile pulled the corners of his mouth downward as he nodded in agreement. "The story of this place, I'm told, is that a massive raid occurred here. These men were not likely Capone's family, but there were many players in the game, and I'm sure his influences could have played a role. The vast tunnel leading away from the estate was found from the outside by law enforcement and defended from the inside by its operators. Now, of course, this was quite a battle of gunfire in the dark that likely led to a face-to-face assault. And so it has been assumed that those men fought each other in the blinding dark to try to bring down this smuggling ring. Of course, with fewer men to surround the main house above, it's assumed that many of these bootleggers held out and then used the tunnels to escape or flank the officers setting the perimeter. The rumor surrounding this history is that those men who gave their lives remain in the tunnel to this day. What was left of the bootleggers took their operations elsewhere and left behind only the many individual bottles and jars that couldn't quickly be removed."

"There is a lot here still. But why the totes? Are you going to take down the racks and do something else with the space? Maybe even 'tear down that wall, Mr. Gorbachev?'" Tanya's laugh at her own joke echoed in the mostly empty space. Her steam of breath blew out in a large cloud and she shivered as she went over and crouched to inspect the totes of booze more closely.

"The plastic is just a modern solution. I don't trust the age of these racks for any sort of practical use," Solomon answered. "I am also not sure if I trust the rest of the cellar to hold up properly if I were to remove such a large piece of wall without a certified contractor to look it over. But then I'd have to trust one to keep any secrets that may be revealed on the other side."

Tanya laughed again with a quick look over her shoulder as she lifted a large labeled bottle to read. "But you trust some strange girl from one of your parties to come down here to listen to your stories and not mention to anyone after leaving that you have a stash of century-old alcohol under your house."

"Well now, I wouldn't say that," Solomon replied in a deep, quiet tone as he loomed over her in the corner.

Tanya stood with the bottle and turned to face Solomon whose sinister expression was shadowed by the twinkling bare bulbs behind him. His body hunched forward as he moved closer. Tanya spoke, "Hey, don't be a creep, alright? I thought we were having a nice time, but now you're too close. I think it might be time for me to go home." When she held up her hands in a defensive posture, she could see the prickling goosebumps on her exposed wrists.

Solomon reached into his pocket and pulled a syringe into view. "Oh, sweet, clever girl. But you are home."

Tanya fumbled to get inside her robe and fetched her handgun with some trouble, only to find the magazine was still removed. She took a wide swing with the bottle in her hand toward Solomon's face but he merely leaned back to avoid it and deftly lunged and wrapped his arm around her neck and positioned himself behind her, holding tight enough to choke her.

The bottle crashed to the floor and scattered glass shards and dark liquid across the cold stone. A sharp pain pricked Tanya's shoulder as Solomon pushed the plunger to dose her. She looked over to see that the needle looked just like one of the drug-filled syringes she kept in her purse.

Solomon let go of her and stood back as she flailed at him with the empty gun only to miss again. His face was cold and patient as he walked over to retrieve the neck of the broken bottle from the floor. "It seems I'll have to have another auction to replace the loss from this unfortunate accident. How much do you believe is a fair price to start the bidding on a bright, radiant young lady like yourself? Shall I call and ask your father? Or perhaps ask your dear sister? I have an idea, why don't you ask her for me?"

Tanya scowled and wobbled on weak knees. She ran toward the stairs as fast as her spinning head would allow and began to climb. The bright bulbs were nearly blinding against the difficulty of blurry vision. They created an intense flare of light like high-beam headlights on a dark, wet road. She fought her way, stumbling up the stairs, until she reached the last step only to meet Mr. Christian waiting for her.

He took a firm hold of one arm to pull her to her feet, forced the gun from her hand, and backed out of the way. He held her for Solomon who came into view in the studio bookcase door as the room features faded with the sunset.

"How do these uppity dilettantes say it, Mr. Christian? We'd be remiss to ignore the most recent feature of our humble abode." Solomon chuckled to himself as he gestured for Mr. Christian to follow.

He led them through the main hall and up the stairs while Tanya made feeble attempts to escape the hold on her arm. Her legs would no longer hold her and she struggled to keep throwing punches at the larger man as she was mostly dragged up the steps. She was brought through a door into a room darkened by a blocked window. Her eyes were heavy and closing as she was brought to the foot of a bed much like the one she slept in the night before. She could see a human figure lying there on top of the blanketing with their arms straight out at either side.

When her chin dropped from exhaustion, she felt a series of

light slaps across her tear-soaked cheek. "No, no, no, Miss Johnston. Not yet," Solomon said. "Plenty of time for that. I couldn't let you slip away from us before you had some explanation of why I can't afford to lose you just yet. How long has it been since you last spoke with Melissa?"

Tanya forced a look at the figure again, focusing on the face. "Missy!" she slurred. "Missy, I'm here! Missy, wake up!"

Chapter Fifteen - Indecent Exposure

Blake turned off the shower water to better hear the thumping on his apartment door.

"Deac, can you get that? Yo, Deac!"

Another loud repeat of knocks rained on the door as Blake fumbled with his towel. One end of the cloth dipped into the commode as he lost his footing and he threw the towel into the tub in frustration. He swore at himself and resigned to answer the knock while dripping and naked.

"Deac, why did you lock the-" Blake stopped himself when he saw DX in the hallway leaning to make room for a woman with sleek black hair wrapped up in a tight bun.

She gave Blake a concerned look and then turned her head. "If I'm interrupting, I can give you a few minutes."

"Agent Waites," Blake confirmed. "What didn't I do this time? I'm sure in your line of work, you're content to catch someone with their pants down. I know you've seen worse," he joked arrogantly, resting a hand across the door header. "But I'm just about to head out, so spill it."

Deacon stifled a laugh and excused himself to get through the door while Blake made room and then blocked the space again as water dripped off his chin and hair.

Agent Waites looked back impatiently. "I just need a few minutes. It's about Louis Carelli."

Blake stood to one side and gestured for her to enter his apartment. He turned to watch and closed the door as Deacon threw a pair of gray sweatpants at him.

As he pulled on his pants, Blake insisted, "Did you go fishing, Deac?"

"Funny... No, it started raining when you jumped in the shower, so I went out to tarp the bikes. Your lady friend here said she knew you and flashed a badge, so here we are," Deacon answered as he filled three plastic cups with tap water to pass out to them.

Waites took a glance around the small apartment living room and stopped next to the wooden arm of Blake's futon. "Normally I'd prefer to speak in confidence, but I don't have time for formalities and I don't care who your friend is. We've been watching one of Carelli's men for some time now."

"I gave testimony to you and the police that I am no longer affiliated with the Carelli family," Blake told her in a flat, rehearsed tone.

"But you were on their payroll for several years, and may recognize a face," Waites interrupted. She pulled a photo from inside her peacoat to show him. "He's about your age and probably would have been working alongside you before the bar turned over to Laurent."

"I don't need a history lesson. A lot of guys worked for Carelli. I unloaded trucks, stocked bottles, and swept up. It was in my best interests to not make friends," Blake said. "Besides, you're talking almost thirty years ago. I was a kid, I got into plenty of my own trouble, not counting the mess I'm in now."

Agent Waites took back the photo to put in her breast pocket. "Your current case is only on hold because a friend of yours submitted evidence, Mr. Gentry. The prosecutor pushed for a continuance to try to tie you to the arsonist. He wants a bigger fish. You knew that when they delayed the investigation to find your partner, who still hasn't emerged. But their time expired on Mr. Laurent, and now they want to try to roll on the family."

"And that's where you come in to help keep the clock ticking, huh?" Blake checked his duffel bag and folded in the costume jacket before zipping it closed. He went to the far side of the futon to a basket of clothes and began to redress himself in jeans and a t-shirt then laid out his riding chaps. "Well, I told you I don't make many friends. What evidence?"

"There was a video recording from a cell phone submitted to your case," Waites added. "Your bike accident and the video cleared you with the judge, so they're pushing this supposed accomplice they believe was working for Carelli."

Blake huffed and pulled on a pair of boots as he leaned against a wall, avoiding her gaze. "Which would roll it back onto me. Yeah, I get it. You're wasting your time here. I don't know your guy or whoever was on that video. I've been playing by the rules, working a second job, living like this, just to get my damn accounts clean and my name back. Don't you think if I were that deep in the weeds I'd have cleared out and started over by now? Six years is a long time to sit around waiting for some weasel attorney to give up on a claims case so I can rebuild before I'm too old to give a shit. What's the statute of limitations for an alleged flight risk on probation?"

Agent Waites walked toward the door. "Alright. I guess I'm wasting my time. For what it's worth, everything you've said so far checks out. But I wouldn't be doing my job if I didn't turn over every stone, right? If I were in your shoes, I might hire a defense lawyer who wasn't also on Carelli's payroll though. His involvement is only keeping the pilot light on against you. Tell the judge you can't afford him, get out of this mess, and make me a believer."

Agent Waites let herself out past Deacon who was sitting in the small kitchen, waiting quietly. When a minute or so passed, he looked up at Blake who was pulling an old, faded leather jacket from a plastic tote in his tiny, mirrored closet. The top rocker patch lettering on the back was still clear and read REGULATORS.

Deacon shook his head in disbelief. "Looks like that thing is a little small on you. Hey, is every woman you know a dime?"

"It may not fit the same, but it's warm, and you said it was raining." Blake zipped the jacket and rolled his neck before shaking a couple of pills into his mouth then replaced the bottle in a drawer. "As for the women, well, Deac, you know how it is. Some things change, and some things don't." He pulled on his gloves and grabbed his helmet and bag. "She's a badge, though. They're only hot when you're guilty."

The bikers shared a laugh and bumped fists as they left the apartment.

**

Fisher returned to Simon, huffing to catch his breath. "This is the only way in. There's some kind of shell or something I can't get through. This tunnel must be far enough underneath to not be affected by whatever this is. On the surface, this was an old mine that was closed off."

"Well, down here, it's a sanctum of some kind," Mama chimed in. "And whatever is keeping us out is doing a damn fine job of it."

Simon peered into the dark space in front of them as if he could concentrate hard enough to make it reveal its secrets. "One way in probably means this is the only way out, too. Do you think it's the same on the other side? Or maybe it's only open here? Sure would have been helpful if Joshua had come."

Mama raised her brow at him and in a soft tone reminded Simon, "We can't hold that boy to any more than he's already been through. If not for him, we would still be out in the cold staring at walls. But if Fisher is right, and it's a mine, it'll only take us farther down under instead of up into the house."

Simon followed her gaze as she looked up on the hill. "It doesn't even look like the same place here. Not like it was, anyway."

Where once was a grand and sturdy Victorian estate, whose exterior was a collaboration of stone and wood framing, now stood a windowless, vine-entangled, moss-mantled structure that swayed and creaked as if it were as easy to move as a thicket of young trees with their branches twisted and fused. A deep fissure down its middle gaped and lapped like a vertical mouth savoring a meal. The eaves drooped in deep stress and splintered as if the entire structure was an elderly man awaiting a visitor. Even its threshold at the base slouched forward in a sort of toothless underbite. The distance between the impassible shell and the decrepit mansion bore a thin veil of blackened, spore-like particles as if one could see dust floating only in the shadowy side of sunlight.

"We came this far," Simon said doggedly. "If we're wrong about this, we'll know soon enough. Just don't go wandering off in there."

Simon led them toward the mineshaft entrance as the earth below their feet cracked in dry protest to their footsteps. Once inside, the darkness crept over with a deep cold. He massaged his jaw and licked his teeth to soothe their chattering as they crept inward. A dull wisp of bluish light swirled ahead of them and then darted toward Simon.

Once it was close, it flew between each face uttering a dry gasping sound, though careful not to touch, and then moved back into the tunnel slowly away from them. When Simon and the others moved forward, the wisp hurried to them again, gagging and gulping for air. But once more it resigned and moved away.

"Do you think this is another one of us? Like my Joshua?" Mama asked. "Is this a lost soul?"

Simon didn't answer but didn't move either. He watched as this light bobbed and when it reached its point of origin, it appeared to split into two. Then three, and more. A sound echoed faintly in the tunnel like a cough, which was joined by others until the echoes carried into silence.

Simon waved Mama and Fisher to follow as he pushed on into the dark. They came to where the lights were milling about and stopped to see they were surrounding a dark stain on the stone floor. Each of these light wisps touched the stain in turn and began to groan and wail until the echoes were growing to a drowning cacophony. The stain slowly dissipated as the lights swirled around faster. They grew larger and brighter and began to bump clumsily like bumblebees into Simon and the others. Their touch was icy and becoming heavier, pushing more forcefully as they grew larger.

Fisher warned, "We can't stay here. Whatever the hell this is is only getting stronger."

"Push through!" Simon ordered as he charged into the lights.

Once he advanced and made contact, the lights pulled back and rallied together and swung into him. His feet left the ground with the impact to his chest and he slid across the crackling dirt. The ground beneath him split apart and a jet of steam shot up between his parted legs. The glowing orbs billowed and joined over the jet where they gulped and grew together as one. A roaring word resounded in the tunnel as Simon felt himself being lifted again, this time by his arms.

"Come on, baby! We can't be here!" Mama shouted against the deafening noise.

Dust crumbled from overhead and obscured their vision as Mama and Fisher carried Simon out into the open. When they escaped the darkness, the impassable shell had become visible in ethereal blue against a starry sky. Stormy clouds began to circle over the mansion and left only a small eye in the center to peek through to the heavens.

"What was that?" Fisher cried as he rubbed his ears.

"Did you hear them?" Simon shook his head.

Mama helped Simon to his feet and he held his ribs. "Hear who, baby?"

Simon repeated, "Did you hear them? Thirst. I think that's what they said. Thirst. The- The puddle! The steam! They were drinking. Did you see they were drinking?"

"Oh baby, I don't know what I saw or what you heard. But I ain't never felt a cold like that." Mama stood in front of him, holding both his hands. "Whatever you think that means, we can't be going back in this way. Just look at this place. Whatever we done just brought down hell! Mama don't remember this part of the scripture."

"We should go back to Joshua," Fisher suggested. He stood with his hands on his head in disbelief. "I've never been good at this trial-by-fire kind of thing, I need to analyze and think."

Simon let go of Mama to grab hold of Fisher's shirt. "We can't go all the way back there. We need to see what's going on here before it's too late. We agreed the pack comes first."

"It does." Fisher put his hand over Simon's and pulled it away. "Joshua is still part of the pack. Maybe he can make this make sense. You guys keep an eye on Sam and Reno. I'll be back as soon as I've got something." Fisher waited until Simon relented with a nod. "This is what I'm good at, remember? I'll figure it out and I'll be back. Trust me."

As Fisher ran off, Mama took Simon's hand and pulled. Together they ripped through the membrane of space between realities and looked up the hill at the sturdy mansion against the twilight sky.

"That boy is gonna be just fine. We taught him just fine." She looked into Simon's eyes and squeezed him tight around his waist. "Come on now, before somebody spots us out here."

Chapter Sixteen - Cheap Shots

A single blinding spotlight shone from the curtain on stage as Blake stepped into its beam. The sounds of screeching tires led into a pounding drum rhythm that mimicked a loud idling motorcycle engine. Blake held his arms high and twisted one fist like he was cranking the throttle on a pair of ape hanger handlebars in the spotlight silhouette. A yellow firework display suspended on either side of the curtain sparked the letters "J" and "R" respectively for the audience to see. The drum beats cut out to the squeal of an electric guitar that slid down the frets like a speeding bike as the rest of the lights came up in the arena to reveal him in his riding leathers, wraparound sunglasses, and fringed and sequined Jerry Riggs costume jacket.

The audience booed him immediately and kept up their indignant protest as he strode down the ramp to enter the ring. He threw a leg over the middle rope and found a cameraman to lean toward. Blake lowered his glasses down to reveal a bandage on his nose and spat gum at the lens of the camera. He leaned back and held the top rope until his wet hair touched the ring apron and pointed straight up until the music hit a downbeat which cued him to gesture a victory pump.

He entered the ring with a bounce in his step, grinning at the disapproving audience. He threw his arms at his sides, curled his fingers, and mouthed the words, "Bring it on!" He reached out through the ropes toward an announce table to fetch a microphone from the commentator standing by.

Blake returned to the center of the ring and brought the microphone to his mouth when Handsome Stan's voice broke in to shout, "Cut the music! Cut the music!"

Blake turned to look as his boss appeared on the stage in a brown suit, already sweating profusely. Stan approached the ring as he spoke through a microphone. "I thought I made it clear to you after your last little stunt that you were indefinitely suspended!" Stan made a quick effort to get into the ring and pulled at his collar to loosen a blue necktie. "This is not the Jerry Riggs Show. In case you didn't know, you ain't calling the shots around here, bub."

Blake yanked off his sunglasses, then threw them out of the ring and answered, "The only shots you're calling are for room service." Blake smiled and let the audience take their time to react. "In fact, I think from the stain on your tie, you've had just about enough."

Again the fans reacted, but with mixed favor and dissent. Stan didn't wait for them to go on. "I want you out of this ring. I don't care what you have to say. No one else here cares what you have to say. And I told you that if you showed up here before your suspension was lifted, I'd toss you out of the building myself if I have to."

Blake gestured directly to Stan to come and get him. He removed his jacket and tossed it between the ropes then raised his mic. "Stan, you couldn't toss a salad. What you can do, for a change, is shut your mouth because I came here tonight to let all these people know that your golden boy, Murphy, ain't gonna be medically cleared to come back any time soon, and that makes me the number one contender. You know it, I know it, and these people know it. There's nobody in that locker room I haven't gone through to get where I am, and I deserve a shot at that lump of gold you call a title belt."

Blake and Stan mouthed off to each other simultaneously without their microphones as they came nose to nose. Stan looked over his shoulder and pointed to the stage for Blake to leave and instead Blake turned his back and postured for the audience. When he returned to face Stan, he pushed him and waved him away. Stan threw down his mic and pushed back. Blake spat at him and slapped Stan's face and grinned again with his arms out in challenge. Stan took a wild swing and Blake ducked under the punch, reached back to grab Stan's neck, and dropped him onto the mat.

Blake popped up on one knee and crawled over toward his boss much the way he had to Murphy at the last show. Before he could get over to Stan, unfamiliar music started and the lights flashed in time with the heavy metal playing. A wrestler in his prime emerged from the curtain, striding to the ring as Blake looked on and slowly stood to invite the man in for a fight.

This man had wild brown hair and a full beard to match. He wore silver shorts and a black t-shirt with white lettering that read, "Endo de Line," with the last word struck out. As Blake stepped closer, Endo propelled himself up to the top rope where he nearly slipped and used it to springboard into a botched flip. Blake had to catch him to protect the other performer but still sold it as a devastating finishing maneuver.

As Blake lay there, the newcomer kipped up to his feet and the crowd again started a chant that said "THIS-IS-BOR-ING."

Blake covered his face and rolled toward Stan to tell him, "They hate it, Stan. What's the plan?"

When Endo helped Stan to his feet and brushed him off, the fans booed again, rejecting the twist in the show. Stan pointed angrily at Blake while making it look like he was giving orders to the new man, but told both wrestlers to set up a cheap shot. He pointed again toward the curtain and told them, "Through the uprights," to call his change of plan on the fly.

Endo nodded, then laughed maliciously in character as he bent over to slap Blake in the back of the head twice. Then he grabbed a handful of Blake's hair to start to pull him up as Stan jumped to face the audience and tried to rally them to cheer. When they only showed disapproval again, Stan turned back to the two wrestlers and, as soon as he got close, Blake threw both his arms up to deliver a cheap shot to each man. They both sold the shot with a shocked look. Stan fell face first and Blake tripped the other man with a leg scissor so that he fell on top of their boss with Endo's face planted in Stan's backside.

The crowd turned their disposition and cheered at the embarrassment of the company's boss and his new protege. Blake made a gesture like he was taking a picture of the scene.

His music struck again with the screeching tire sound and he rolled down under the bottom rope to exit, remembering to hold his neck to sell the blockbuster neckbreaker that wrecked the spot.

When he had left and walked out of the spotlight through the curtain, he was met quickly by a pony-tailed and bespectacled man with a clipboard wearing a headset. Before he could speak, Blake put his hands up in defense.

"Yeah, yeah, I know, Freddie. We just scrapped your whole genius buildup for the next few weeks."

"Weeks?" Freddie screamed and threw his clipboard. "Months, at least! Dammit, Gentry, what am I supposed to do with that kid now?"

"Hey, I don't know. But he could've been hurt slipping that rope," Blake explained. "Stan made the call when I was supposed to be selling, so I did what I was told."

The producer pulled side to side on his tie and settled his weight on one leg as his toe tapped. "That's the business, though, ain't it? Heads are gonna roll to try to make a 50-year-old biker with bad knees a star, you know?"

"Slow down, Freddie!" Blake laughed. "Not even 45 yet. I'll work with you guys. You know it'll be alright. I'll just play a 'me against the boss' angle or something for a few weeks until Murphy gets back or whatever you want." Blake pulled the tape off his nose and tweaked it.

"We'll call ya," Freddie said with a dismissive wave. "I still gotta get through the rest of the night. Hell, this was just the curtain jerker."

Blake cracked his knuckles and started to unwind the tape from his hand. "Well, maybe now I'll be able to keep up with those damn fines on time," he laughed to himself.

***

When night fell, Simon and Mama worked their way close to the house to observe the scanning security cameras and motion-detecting lights. After finding a pattern, they decided to keep cover in some low coniferous hedges. Unsure of whether the devices recorded sound, they whispered together.

"You've already been inside the house, so we know we can get in. But both of us would be riskier than one," Simon said. "I'll give a signal every time the cameras pass so that when you come back out you'll know you can make your move. At least if we know where Sam and Reno are, we can try to get them out. Or if they-"

"They're in there," Mama assured with a stern look. "I can feel it, they're still with us, baby."

Simon put up a finger over the hedge to show Mama the cameras had moved and she darted toward the hanging curtain of plastic on the patio. Once she made it inside the house, Simon lost sight of her in the darkened main hall. Now all he could do was wait and try not to think the worst.

Simon caught sight of a pair of men in the house that were merely shadows, one a bit thicker and taller than the other. He could scarcely hear their voices and the flapping plastic curtain made it too difficult to catch whole words. He did not raise his finger signal for several passes of the cameras while the men were in sight, for fear Mama might see and give herself away.

He lost track of the men after they passed a section between windows where he couldn't see, and he threw up his signal as promised. He repeated this action and carefully watched for an amount of time he couldn't track. Mama finally reemerged and slid behind the bushes out of breath.

"There were just two men in that house right now that I could see," Mama whispered. "So they took a minute to get around." Simon balled up his fists impatiently. "But wait now. I found them. They're locked up in a big old safe that's built into a corner. It's got a keypad lock and one of those men has the code. But they fine, for now. Sam tells me they been watched and starved but for water. And that they supposed to be part of some kinda sideshow bullshit. Some kind of sport for these people, like they gonna make them fight each other at their next party."

"Dammit!" Simon ground his teeth angrily.

"Hush now, baby. We doin' better than we were yesterday," Mama said to calm him. "Let's get on back away from these cameras so we can meet Fisher. If we can't get that code, that safe is gonna stay locked."

148

Chapter Seventeen - A Guest is a Pest

The nightmare continued pulling Melissa through the recesses of her consciousness. With its shifting planes and visceral illusions, the one constant vision that kept coming back was the face that looked almost like her own. The voice that feebly begged her over and over.

"Missy, wake up! Missy, I'm here."

Mass and gravity were fluid catalysts to her stirring version of reality. The suns, while no longer appearing directly, remained a burden that bore toward her like a vice. Colors came and went in phases similar to drowning one moment and gasping for air the next. She could neither predict the currents nor fight the waves, and still could not simply close her eyes and separate herself from this environment.

A shadow had appeared a few times that seemed benevolent somehow. He was condescending in his posture and kept his eyes hidden, though his features were masculine and his hair a tangle of curling black. Always he walked away and left Melissa unsure if he was guiding or leaving, yet he managed to be visible in some way to her, whether just out of reach or traversing the horizon.

She would step into a room only to be surrounded by nothing and unable to touch something sturdy to balance herself. Walls might build in front of her eyes as easily as melt, or even devour each other. Or she'd see the light of a flame gather with other flames and rush toward her only to splash into sparks just before her hesitation would pitch her body upward or backward or any which way, leaving her to brace for the surge of new images or landscapes.

It could all move and change so quickly at times, yet other scenes were agonizingly long with no concept of how much time might be passing, or if it did at all.

That face appeared again. That woman. She came into view only as a face each time, like an angel of death warning that stillness and complacency would be Melissa's ultimate end. That despite the futility of the dreamscape, being still would not serve her.

Melissa took an overconfident step that gave out beneath her and her body reeled and contorted into a void so swallowed by darkness that she couldn't see the unforgiving solid masses that her body struck and slammed into. Each of these would alter the direction of her movements and fling her limbs about until the whole of her body was beaten and wounded and infested and withering with atrophy.

Another illusion appeared close enough to take hold. It was a scroll of star shine that burned to the touch but she held fast and climbed desperately as her elbows and knees seared and sizzled. The scroll unwound away upward until it emptied and burst into a fetid gas. Melissa held her lips tightly closed until the mist swarmed and forced its way in and swelled her chest with rot.

"Missy, I'm here," came the voice again. It was almost a

whisper this time though her head pounded like a cathedral bell.

She had no voice to respond as she gagged and gasped in silent screams. The whispered woman's voice slowly grew louder, echoing back over and over, growing louder until Melissa's body crashed against a narrow ledge of fungal earth. She clung to it as another wave of color washed around her as if she had taken only a few steps through the room from which she fell.

When she saw the step that fell away replace itself, the shadow man came with it and walked off casually through the arched doorway of the room with no walls.

***

Tanya's body was twisted in the bedsheets. She struggled to even lift her arms to rub her aching muscles. She was exhausted and her vision was hazy as a steady pounding sound made it harder to open her eyes. She pulled herself to the edge of the bed to see a large, blurry figure swinging a hammer.

As the figure came into focus as Mr. Christian, Tanya's stomach turned and she vomited onto the hardwood floor. She held her head with a great deal of difficulty with such heavy arms but managed to cover her face with a pillow to try to muffle the sounds and smells of the dark room.

When she lifted her head, the man was gone and a dull light barely crept in through the edges of the shutter louvers. Her vision was clearer now and she was thankful for the quiet. She pressed a cramped hand to her chest and tried to breathe deeply. There was a lingering smell of vinegar and she looked to see the spot where she had vomited was as clean and shining as any other portion of the floor.

With some effort, she pulled back the sheet and blanket. Tanya shivered at the cold and felt she had been stripped of her clothing. Her hair was a mess that hung partially over her eyes, and the bile taste that stuck to her lips had her gulping for something to drink. On weakened knees and using short, careful steps, she slowly made her way to the bathroom while hugging her naked body to combat the chill.

She made it to the doorway and felt for a light switch. The light from the bright white bulb made her flinch and slap at the switch to turn it off. Pink spots pervaded her sight as she blinked to adjust. Tanya grabbed the edge of the sink to steady herself then cranked the faucet to splash water on her face. She cupped more into her mouth to rinse and spit and then drink. She ran her fingers through her tangled hair and pulled at the strands that stuck together. Once she could see better, she noticed and reached for a fluffy, oversized robe that hung on the open door. As she was pulling on the sleeves, she caught sight of the bruising on her shoulder and the memory of Solomon stabbing the needle into her came flooding back.

She reached for another handful of cold water, then rubbed it against her sore shoulder and cried out as she applied pressure. She rushed back out into the room and tried the doorknob in vain. She rattled it again as if it might give. Then she strangled the knob with both hands before pounding on the door. She screamed out in frustration with a ragged, strained voice.

She turned her back against the door and slid down to sit while holding her face. Tanya's eyes were again drawn to the peeking light at the window and she crawled her way to it. She stood to see the shutters had been drawn, padlocked, and nailed shut.

Tanya heard a key in the door and bit back the urge to scream. She almost fell on her way to the door, using the bedpost to hold herself upright as it opened.

"Good morning, Miss Johnston," Solomon grinned.

He and Mr. Christian came through the door carrying a small table and placed it just inside the room then brought in two chairs. Tanya attempted to escape while they were setting the table, but Mr. Christian stepped in her way with his thick arms crossed. His proud chin stared down at her as she scrambled to stay standing and weakly threw her fists at him. He easily restrained her and walked her back into the room.

"You're not well," Mr. Christian said with a tone of sympathy as if he were trying to help her. "You should sit and have something to eat. You need your strength."

Solomon left the room and returned from the hallway with a small cart. From it, he unfolded a cloth to dress the table and placed a serving dish between two plates.

153

"Please have a seat." Solomon held a chair for her.

Mr. Christian lifted the lid of the serving dish to reveal a steaming stack of pancakes. From the cart, he brought a large bowl covered in a napkin that he revealed to be filled with various fruits.

Tanya refused the chair offered to her and went to the other one to sit. She glared at both men for a long moment until Solomon rolled up his shirt sleeves and sat. He reached for a few pancakes and began to remove the peel from a banana. He wrapped the fruit in a pancake and took a bite then looked hopefully at Tanya to join him.

She looked at the window and bed and the doorway behind Mr. Christian and then back to the table. She fidgeted a moment and then stuffed a handful of berries into her mouth. She began tearing pieces of a pancake apart to eat and grabbed for an orange.

With a mouthful of food, she remarked sarcastically, "You have this great big house and no fork and knife for your 'guests'."

"In your current state, I felt it best to have a meal that doesn't require utensils. Perhaps once you're feeling more yourself." He took another bite and asked, "I was hoping you could tell me another story. Maybe one about you and your sister."

Tanya avoided his eyes. They were soft, just like before he drugged her. She rubbed her shoulder gently and cut into her orange with her fingernails to split it in half. "I'd much rather we didn't talk. My stomach is upset enough without your voice giving me a headache," she muttered.

"Alright. I can grant that wish if you like. Just keep in mind that any privileges you have in my home will depend on your behavior," he warned gently. "And right now, you're being quite rude."

As if his words were a command to Mr. Christian, the larger man stepped forward and picked up the table with the tray and plates and carried it to the door to push it out into the hallway. Tanya grabbed at the stack of pancakes only for Solomon to smack her fingers and then take what was left of the orange out of her hands. He left the room and Mr. Christian came back for the chairs. He upturned the one Tanya sat on and poured her onto the floor. He left the room with Solomon reaching in to close the door behind them.

As the key jammed into the lock, Tanya screamed at the door until her throat hurt.

She had exhausted herself to sleep on the floor but was awoken just as abruptly. Solomon entered the room again, this time bringing only a bowl of water and a loaf of bread. He set these on the bedside table and held out his hand to help Tanya to her feet. She couldn't tell how much time had passed, but thin rays of sun trying to peek through the tight shutters indicated it was daytime.

"Spending hours on this floor is not good for your back, Miss Johnston. Breakfast was disappointing, but I thought it best to give you an opportunity to redeem yourself over a light lunch."

She refused his hand and pushed herself up on her elbows. He lingered until she crawled toward the bed and then he turned to close the door.

"You really do need to eat something. Come now and sit up to eat. If you mind your manners, I'll let you choose what we have for supper. How's that sound?"

Tanya climbed up onto the bed until she was within reach of the bowl. She lifted it to her lips and drank. Then she scooped a handful to splash on her face. She dried with the sleeve of her robe and reached for the bread. "Where are my clothes?" she croaked.

"Ah, she speaks! Yes, I took them for cleaning after your unfortunate sickness. They are ready for you once you've earned them," he promised. "I'm sure you're plenty cold enough to want them back."

"I don't understand what you want from me. From either of us." Tanya tore the bread loaf into bite-sized pieces. "How long has Missy been here like... like that?"

"Now, now, be a good guest. My question first and then I'll answer one for you." Solomon paced around the bed and straightened the pillows. "Did you come here for your sister?"

Tanya weighed the question and began her answer more than once. "Well, no. I mean, yes. What I mean is, I didn't know she was here, but I was looking for her."

"Now that sounds like it shouldn't have been so difficult to answer." His voice reminded her of a condescending principal. When Tanya began to argue, he held up his hand. "No need to fuss. It's okay, I believe you. You've been looking for a long time, then. How long has she been a monster?"

Tanya stood suddenly and choked on a mouthful of bread until she felt she had to sit again. She gagged and waved her hands hysterically until her breath caught. She took another long drink from the bowl and a cough brought most of her mouthful of crumbs out into the water.

"Let's not get too excited," he smiled with feigned sympathy. "But it's true, and I find acceptance helps us begin to learn. How long have you known she is a… what she is?"

Tanya caught her breath with a shiver and stared at the bowl of floating breadcrumbs. She pulled a pillow into her lap and tucked her legs up on the bed. "Why does that matter? What do you want with her?"

"Miss Johnston, you're not playing nice. It's not your turn."

She pulled in a slow, deep breath and looked into his eyes to challenge him. "If you're going to keep me here, I need some socks. Some warm clothes."

Solomon leaned on one knee and reached to push her hair out of her eyes. She flinched away from his reach. "And what do I get in return?" His smile softened as he tilted his head as if he could see her better this way. "I would appreciate some manners. You could speak when spoken to instead of trying to get one over on me. The sooner you accept your situation, the sooner we can conclude our time together."

Tanya rubbed her hands and brought them to her face. She pushed her hair out of her eyes and carefully sat up against the headboard. "I thought I lost her a few years ago. And what friends I had then told me to let her go but I couldn't. And now that I'm closer than I've been since then, I feel like I'm farther away than ever in my life."

"This may not be of any consolation to you. But I am not keeping her to HURT you. I'm keeping you to CONTROL her. To better answer your question, I've hired her to be here for my entertainment. You might be interested to know she was working at a seedy kink club when I found her."

Tanya raised a judgmental eyebrow. "I think that says more about you than it does her. A girl's got to eat."

"I see you still have your sense of humor. Why hunt for your prey when a vampire can bring the prey to herself and have them pay for the experience?" Solomon took stock of her stunned and defeated expression before he stood up and took the bowl in to rinse. He refilled it with cold water and returned. "I'm not in a position to look down on anyone's profession. She's earning honestly. Not everybody wants to get shot at for a living." He reached into his pocket for two tablet pills. "These should help ease your stomach, if you need them. Those little needle cocktails you brought here clearly weren't meant for you and I'd like to know why you brought them to my little party."

Tanya swallowed hard but tried to hide it with a deep shrug. "I have a, uh, friend who deals. He said it works better than pepper spray if some creep gets all over me."

"And the handgun for buying time until the drugs set in, most likely," Solomon chuckled. "Because something tells me you don't really want to shoot anyone. See, now we're opening up so nicely. I'll lay out something for supper and make sure you have something to wear. I'm having a little gathering tonight and I insist that you join us. There's a bar of soap and a towel in the bathroom. I'll be back in a few hours."

"Wait! You can't just keep me locked up in here!"

"Is that right?" Solomon asked. "Well, during your stay here, I'll make you a little deal. If you can take the key to this room, I won't make any effort to stop you from leaving." Before he closed the door, he turned. "Although I'm afraid Mr. Christian will not be a part of this agreement and he is less patient than I am."

Chapter Eighteen - Biding Time

Simon came to a long, paved lane lined with evenly spaced black gum trees. Their bare branches reached out to each other but were unable to touch. He looked up between them to see the storm clouds that had started to gather in the night were billowing.

The large white house came into view and spurred him to run the last leg of the driveway. It was somewhat unclean from years of neglect and weather. He pulled the key from his pocket again and tried the lock. The jamb stuck at first but gave under force and he pushed the door wide open.

The inside was nearly immaculate. Many of the rooms were furnished but undisturbed. He hurried through the house to see what he could find of use, noting a fireplace downstairs. In only one of the upstairs bedrooms, there was a full closet of clothing for a thin man.

"Well, I'll be damned. I owe him one for this," Simon muttered with an apologetic tone to the empty house.

He pulled on a heavy sweater from the closet whose threads pulled tight at the shoulders. He returned to the ground floor to look for food but couldn't find even a can of soup. There were also no dishes of any kind, yet there were cleaning chemicals under the sink.

Simon stepped out on the front porch where he saw some

deer on a nearby hill. Hunger and instinct took over, and he was soon transformed and on the chase. His paws pounded as he gave chase and closed the gap between them. He brought down the buck and stopped over the body to howl out for Mama and Fisher to hear.

While waiting for the others to answer his call, Simon dragged the deer closer to the white house and began to snap branches from the first tree on the row for firewood. He had time to stack a healthy pile of wood before the others arrived.

"You got good timing, baby," Mama huffed as she and Fisher reached the house. "We were just about to come hunting for ya."

Fisher nodded over Mama's shoulder. "Those guys moved Sam and Reno. By the time we saw them doing it, we couldn't get to them. They're locked up in that little panic room the owner dropped outside the other morning. God, what day is it, anyway?"

Simon exchanged looks with his pack and slammed down a stack of branches. He looked around wildly for a moment and had to calm himself. "Are they okay? Is it another keypad lock?"

"They're alive," Mama said. "After they slammed the door, we got on up close and sniffed around. I guess those assholes ain't watching, or don't care if a big dog come around. So I hugged up against it and made sure they weren't hurt. They got them knocked out somehow."

Fisher chimed in, "Drugged food most likely. Like tranquilizers. With the limited visibility from the trees, we just couldn't get to them fast enough to intervene."

Fisher picked up a pile of the branches and took them inside when Simon nodded toward the open door.

Simon pulled a broad knife and made his way back to the deer to begin the dressing process. He waved Mama over to help where she could. "It's not his fault."

"You should tell him that yourself, you know? He looks up to you."

"He's been making better decisions than I have lately," Simon admitted. "Did he get anything useful from his time with Joshua?"

"Nah. He says our Joshua ain't making no sense. Something about the shifting current drowning in spirit. Says we can't see in the storm for the eye. But that sounds backward to me. Maybe I ain't saying it right." Mama stood up with a shiver and watched the trees bend in the new wind.

Simon stopped to follow her eyes and then watched her hugging herself in the cold. "There's a closet upstairs. I doubt anything will fit quite right, but we can make do until Fisher gets a fire going. I'll go talk to him while you put on something warm."

Mama looked back at him and bowed her head. "Just tell me we're gonna all be together again soon. Lie to me if you have to, but I need convincing. Tell me that leaving them there is just til we can get warm enough to go get my babies out of that prison."

Simon took her in his arms and held her. "Maybe what Joshua said makes sense. This storm is gonna be a bad one, Phie. We're going to go back stronger, able to see better. And get them free so we can be together in this big house my brother sent us to. THIS is where I was supposed to bring us. And if this snow is as bad as I think it's going to be, Blake may have just saved us so we can bring them here soon too. I can't wait to hear Reno complain that the house is too white."

Mama laughed through the tears on her face. "You could build a house exactly as he planned and that boy would find something wrong with it. He always wants better. You taught him that, baby." She laid a hand on Simon's face and gave it a gentle smack. "Come on now, before you get to thinking we need to go back before this storm puts down."

***

Blake finished a call to Sgt. Gordy as a knock came at the door. He called out, "It's open."

Mo opened the door but Gia burst in past him toward Blake, who had his feet propped up and was wearing only a pair of gray sweat pants. "He doesn't believe me, so maybe I can talk some sense into you."

"I guess this isn't a wellness check. What are you doing here?" Blake asked.

Mo was about to close the door when DX came in behind them.

"I wasn't expecting a party," Blake joked.

Gia threw her hands up. "I go to talk to my brother about his date and he tells me that her store was robbed! And neither of you could pick up a phone to tell me that you knew? Have either of you tried to find her? Do you think I don't care what happens to my friends?"

Deacon chimed in, "Maybe they thought you might overreact?"

Gia's eyes narrowed and she squared up to Deacon until she was almost touching his chest and staring up at him. "You ain't seen nothing yet if you think THIS is overreacting."

"Gia, come on," Mo said, pulling her back. "Would you just tell him?" After an awkward moment, he sighed and sat in the chair at the table. "Gia called Tanya and overheard some guy in the background."

"Alright? So what's the big deal?" Blake asked as he lit a cigarette. He sat up on the futon and moved a magazine on the side table to pull over an ashtray.

Gia huffed as she turned from Deacon to face Blake, "The big deal is that ever since the call, her phone's been off, then her shop gets broken into, and I want to go see if she's okay."

"I guess you have some reason to think she's not okay?"

Mo broke in, "It's not like we even know where she is to-"

"Actually, I do, thanks to you," Gia said. "You remember when my car broke down and I didn't have an address, and you said you just used an app on your phone to find me? Well, I wrote down the address of the last location that pinged on her phone. She sounded like she was about to give it up to this guy, and not that it's anybody's business, but he would be her first if she did."

Deacon was amused at the admission and Mo's eyes widened with surprise. When they met Blake's gaze, he shot confused looks back to all three people standing in his kitchen.

Blake shrugged with his hands out. "Isn't that a good thing? I'm still missing something, I guess."

Gia rolled her eyes with a frustrated huff. "She told me about this place she was going to go get a drink, and I think maybe that's where she met him. So I went by there when she didn't answer her phone, and her car was still there. So this guy she's with must have driven her, and based on what Gilly tells me, she drinks too damn much. So I was gonna either help her celebrate or give her a shoulder if it didn't go well."

Deacon cleared his throat. "Do you mean that private bar? Needs a password?"

"What do you know about it?" Gia spun on him again.

"Hey, lay off with the attitude, chica. I know because she invited me there. Your girl asked me on a date, but I was late

165

to meet her and couldn't read the password on the card she gave me." Deacon folded his riding gloves into his belt and smoothed his hair. "I didn't stick around to see her leave. I thought it might be creepy for a big Puerto Rican biker to hang around some quiet little bar like that. And it's too cold to just be sitting outside anyway."

Mo puffed up his chest and let out a long breath during a delayed blink of impatience. He asked Gia, "You said you know where she is? What's the address?"

Gia pulled up a screenshot on her phone and passed it to him. She turned back to Blake. "You know the area pretty good, right? Do you know that west side golf course where the rich houses are? That country club?"

"Yeah, sure. I like to ride up that way in the summertime. It's one of the few roads around here that isn't always under construction. It's not too far."

"Well, that's where she was when I called." Gia sat on the futon next to Blake. "I want to be happy for her if I'm wrong, ya know? But something in my gut says the rest is all bad news. The car, the break-in, and some rich asshole up on a golf course keeping her there like he owns her or something. No way she just shuts off her phone and disappears for a couple of days-"

"Unless she eloped," Deacon suggested. The other three turned to him at the same time. "What? Hey, it happens. And all but the shop getting trashed, it might just be legit. I mean, what more could a girl want than to be swept off her feet by some wealthy dude? Maybe he flies her off to the tropics, they'll have some rum runners on a white sandy beach, and he offers her an easy life on a platter. Then she'll come home in a few weeks, show off her big diamond, and tell you all about it."

Gia stood up again and curled her lip at Deacon. "I think maybe you watch too many telenovelas. If anybody in this room really thinks that Tanya would just run off and get married to some guy that she never told her best friend about, then maybe you won't mind driving me up there to find out? If the house is empty, I'll back off and let her come home and tell me all about it. But if it ain't, then I'm trusting my gut and calling the police."

Mo stood up and got close to her face. "And tell them what, Gia? That she's been kidnapped?"

"You're goddamn right, I will! You watch all those stupid crime shows. After twenty-four hours, you can file a missing persons report and get them on the case." Gia was fuming, her chest heaving, and pointing a finger into her brother's face. "Don't stand there and act like you think she's fine."

"Hold on a minute," Blake stood up and got between them. "Let's not fight here. I just don't understand why you needed to bring this here to me."

"If my brother won't go up there, I thought I could convince you." Gia faced him and softened her expression like it was sure to get what she wanted.

167

"Well, I'm not saying I don't believe you. But," Blake propped a foot up on the arm of his futon to reveal his ankle monitor. He reached for his cigarette pack as he continued. "I'm in no position to go sniffing around some country club. If I get fifty feet outside my building without permission, I go into the clink."

Gia looked at his monitor and held a deep breath. Then she turned a sympathetic look to Mo. "Gilly, please? I'll buy you gas and dinner. Just drive me up there. I'll knock on the door and say we're lost because of the storm."

"So now you think she's been kidnapped, and you're just gonna go knock on his door, and then what?" Mo could see she wasn't going to budge. "Whatever. You owe me dinner and gas. But you aren't gonna knock on his door. We're just gonna go see if there's a car in the drive, and if any lights are on. That's it. Alright?" When Gia nodded, he handed her his keys. "You can start paying me back by starting the car and clearing the snow off. It's been coming down all morning. If we go now, we can get home before the worst of this storm comes in."

Gia hugged him and grabbed the keys to run out the door. Blake approached Mo with a serious look.

"Hey, before you go, I need to tell you something. My brother came looking for me before I saw the shop window. He said he ran into some trouble up there."

"Simon? SIMON has trouble up there?" Mo's eyes went wide.

"I didn't want her to hear it. I was gonna drop you a text if you left at the same time. Just… Don't get out of your car up there. If you can help it, don't even stop the car. I sent him up there to check out a place to lay low. A place on my books that's tied to my court case. I'll text you the address so you can steer clear of it in case that's where he is now." Blake turned around to show the scarred scrape on his lower back. "From my last run-in with Simon when he came to accuse me of setting up his pack. Apparently, one or two of them got snatched by somebody living at the golf course."

"What the-?"

"I know. Trust me, I know." Blake stopped him. "It doesn't make any sense. And I can't go snooping around for myself. If I know Gia, you won't be able to get out of going. But you can keep her in the car and at least be aware."

"No, you don't know." Mo pushed his lips together and looked between the two bikers. "I should tell you, the address Gia just showed me… I went up there a couple of days ago." He hesitated and then confided, "With Agent Waites."

"With Waites?" Blake's face turned red. "What are you doing with Waites?"

"That lady cop?" Deacon asked.

Mo looked at his phone when it chimed and shrugged. "I don't have a lot of time to explain. Gia's waiting."

"Did you just tell me you're a rat?" Blake grabbed the chair between them and threw it across the room, then grabbed Mo's collar and held him with Blake's lit cigarette hanging out of his mouth smoldering close to Mo's face. "You're in bed with the feds? Is that why you ain't been around a long while? Then turn up just when I got things figured out? Are you watching me? Are you the reason my case is still on hold?"

Mo dropped his phone. "Hold up! B, hold up! It ain't like that. Ever since I gave Waites that video of the club arson, she helped me get myself together, like going back to school and getting some contractor jobs for security companies. They bring me in to help with some computer stuff."

Blake let go and snubbed out his smoke. He was seething as he tied his hair up and turned back. He and Deacon exchanged looks and he took a long breath, shaking his head. "That delay is keeping me on a leash. It better have been worth it."

Mo bent to pick up his phone and put it away, ignoring another chime. "I'm sorry if what I did hurt you, man. I was trying to help. I swear to God, I'm in your corner. Mind if I get a puff real quick? This shit is kinda heavy."

Blake lit another one for himself and tossed the pack and lighter to Mo.

Mo lit one and spoke through a gagged breath. "It's been a minute since I smoked. Anyway, her partner is running undercover on a sting operation. This wig up there is throwing around a lot of money, and the ATF thinks he's getting it from selling some illegal hooch."

170

"And how did that put YOU in the house?" Deacon asked.

"This guy ordered a bunch of new security to be delivered. Never has his name on the bill but the address belongs to him, so she asked me to put on a jacket and go in with her to have a quick look at the cameras to see if we can tap into them remotely." There was an awkward pause while Mo took a long, shaky drag and blew a smoke ring. "Hey, I still got it. Sorry, I know it's neither the time nor place. So this hardware is expensive stuff, motion detectors, face recognition. He's not very discreet, probably because he's got someone else signing for everything. Big guy with a big background. We've been looking into it, but we didn't find enough to get a warrant. The owner even gave Waites a case of his stuff to turn over as evidence. It was some cheap knockoff with a bad label. She thinks it's his cover."

Blake blew a large cloud from both nostrils. "Big background, huh? Like mine? She came here out of the blue wanting me to get a new lawyer. Am I still on the hook?"

Deacon moved closer and Blake waved him back.

"I don't know about any of that. She told me the video was helpful, but it pissed off the prosecutor for some reason. The background on this goon is military in an outfit overseas, but I didn't get a look at his file. So Waites assumes the guy he serves was in the same outfit." His phone rang in his pocket. "Look, I gotta go so she'll get off my back. I'll fill you in on more later if you need."

"You want me to ride up there with them?" Deacon asked.

"No, no. Don't do that," Mo answered with his hands up. "She'll just freak out about you creeping on us."

"I wasn't asking you," Deacon gritted out.

Blake shook his head. "Deac, did you see it coming down out there?"

Deacon shrugged, "Hey bro, I told you. If I gotta go somewhere, a little bit of slip ain't gonna stop me."

Blake looked back at Mo. "Tell her she convinced me, and that Deacon going to check it out is as good as me going. It'll be fine. I wish I could get a look at the place. You still got a dash cam?"

"Yeah. It's always on when I drive. I can even livestream to you," Mo confirmed.

Blake sauntered to the kitchen to pull open the fridge. "Good enough for me. Be careful."

Chapter Nineteen - Tainted with Blood

Tanya stood on tip toes to try to see through the narrow slats of the window shutters when she heard multiple cars coming up the driveway. Although she couldn't get a look down at them, she heard what must have been at least a dozen or so parking in the small lot.

She pulled her robe tight and moved to the door to listen just in time to hear the heavy footsteps that belonged to Mr. Christian. The key turned in the door and he entered brusquely with an arm out for Tanya to keep her distance. In the other arm, he held a pile of neatly folded clothes topped with a pair of simple, black flat shoes.

"I'll be back in a few minutes to escort you to the party, Miss Johnston." He placed the clothes on the bedside table and turned to leave.

"Wait! You don't have to keep me here. I want to see my sister," she pleaded as he closed and locked the door. She pounded her fists against it and screamed. "Let me go!"

When he was away from the door, Tanya rushed to the bathroom to pull on a seashell sconce that she noticed to be crooked after her shower. The sconce had curved corners, but they were thin and might help to cut through or break something if she could get it off the wall. With all her might, she had managed to get it to wiggle a bit after a few minutes. The screws held tight against her efforts and she quickly grew tired.

She went to pull on the clothing that was sure to be warmer than the robe and found a pair of blue jeans that were a size too large, the legs too long, and gathered with a crinkle at her ankles. No underwear was provided, but the plain t-shirt and pink wool sweater were a welcome sight even though they also hung oversized on her small frame. The flat shoes pinched her uncomfortably but otherwise fit. She drew a long breath of relief for her cold aching feet to have some layer between her skin and the bare floor.

The door pushed open again as Tanya rolled the waistband of her jeans to keep them from drooping. Mr. Christian stood in the doorway wearing a tuxedo and a dull, gray fez. He extended his arm to her.

Tanya quipped, "Nice hat. If anything, it makes you even more creepy than usual."

"You can come along nicely, or be drugged and dragged again if you like. It's all the same to me." He pulled a syringe from his jacket pocket with a smug grin. "I don't recommend another dose so soon, though. If you behave yourself, I'll make sure you get to join in on the refreshments tonight instead of your usual tap water from a bowl."

"What if you just let me go? You don't have to follow orders. You could just leave the door open and tell him I slipped away and ran for it."

"Oh, I don't recommend running. You'll be exhausted in less

than two minutes and Mr. Solomon is a gifted marksman. Besides, ten minutes ago, you were screaming to get out. Tonight may be your only chance to prove you can be trusted to leave your room."

"You're saying I could earn the right to some freedom?" Tanya asked with surprise.

"Mr. Solomon had me install a very sophisticated security system. You'll be watched at all times but, otherwise, we believe that you deserve some room to move around so long as you can respect the rules of the house."

Tanya took his arm and he lay a broad, strong hand on her wrist. He gave an approving nod and walked them toward the stairs. She held her ground at the top of the stairs.

"Wait," she pleaded. "Can I see her for just a minute before we go down to the party? I promise I won't make a fuss, but I just want to see my sister."

"I'll discuss that with Mr. Solomon. If he agrees, I'll take you to her after the party."

Tanya hesitated and looked across the balcony to the closed door. She looked back at Mr. Christian who patiently waited. With a reluctant nod, she went along with him.

He took her down behind the bookcase into the cellar, following the bright string of lights along the curved stairs. The sounds of voices carried toward her and mixed with the distant sound of Melissa's voice. Was it really her, or was it in her head? She looked back up the stairs as if she might see her sister there somehow. She shook her head as if trying to shake away the sounds just before they entered the large room of the cellar.

In a layered circle, the familiar faces of Solomon's party guests were gathered, all but one wearing matching gray fezzes. The one without was a mostly bald man with glasses that Tanya remembered as the "new money" but couldn't recall a name. He stood in the center of the circle smiling nervously back at the chanting circles of men and Anna May, the only other woman, all dressed to the nines.

The group swayed gently and whispered a chant with their eyes closed. Tanya couldn't make out the words even though they were spoken in unison. Mr. Christian led Tanya to the far side of the room near the plank door where they stood to wait. Solomon revealed himself by speaking another language, or perhaps eloquent gibberish, like hearing a church pastor speaking in tongues for the first time. The others continued muttering in a whisper, almost inaudible if not for the eery echo of the stone walls.

Solomon held a hand high and uttered a shout that silenced the rest of the room at once. In his hand, he held a bottle like the one Tanya had smashed on the floor. As he did, the members of his party each raised a hand with their palms facing upward and placed their other hands on the shoulder of the guest next to them, creating joined concentric rings of people, these cultists, as if it had been rehearsed.

Solomon spoke again, in plain English. "Friends, we have

gathered again to share a taste of our bounty with Mr. David Sterling. After just a sip of our unearthed spirits, he will begin to discover truths about himself on the path to prosperity and enlightenment, just as each of you has done before him. Please speak the words with me as he takes the first drink that will deliver him from darkness."

Solomon lifted a white scarf for everyone to see and requested that Sterling remove his glasses. He then tied the scarf to cover Sterling's eyes and handed him the bottle. "Only a taste, my friend, and we will bring you to the door to take your first steps."

Tanya shifted in place and hugged herself from a sudden chill as the circles of cult members recited in unison,

"Take with thee this night, guide thine eyes without sight.
Soak thine flesh from within, may thee unburden thy sin.
Test thy will by trial, forsaking beholden denial.
May blood-tainted spirits wake, thirst of thine soul to slake."

Sterling held the bottle with both hands and raised it as if accepting a toast by himself. As he tilted it toward his lips, the dark glass of the bottle illuminated a muted blue from within. Sterling wiped his lips with his forearm and held the bottle up again for Solomon to take from him.

The mob made a celebratory grunt and opened the circle toward the plank door where Tanya stood. Sterling, led by Solomon, walked toward her while Mr. Christian pulled the door open to a pitch-dark tunnel. Sterling took his next steps with uncertainty into the darkness and Mr. Christian closed the door behind him. Solomon handed the bottle to the nearest fez-adorned cultist who took a sip between their words and passed it along like a church communion.

The cultist group kept still and began whispering again. Tanya's head throbbed. She backed away from the door and into Mr. Christian who held her there to watch the dark opening with them for a painfully long time. Melissa's voice came again, louder than the echoes, and begged Tanya to find her. She closed her eyes tight and tried to block out all the voices.

The wooden plank barrier slightly muffled the sounds of Sterling's fearful screams and pleas for help over and over. Tanya looked to Solomon whose expression was fixed with a terrifying delight while Mr. Christian kept her facing the simple door. She couldn't help but cry silently at Sterling's wails of anguish. She flinched with empathy as each wail came as though she were being struck with the pain he was enduring.

Solomon and Mr. Christian shared a look when the sounds had quieted. The bodyguard released Tanya and turned to go up the stairs.

Solomon stood beside Tanya before turning to face his guests. The people, who before had circled the center, now formed lines against the wall near the steps with a small gap in the middle where Mr. Christian departed. Solomon raised his hand with his palm upturned and the rest did as well, as if in salute.

Solomon announced with pride and delight, "Gather yourselves, my friends. We have much to discuss and a celebration to prepare. Let us retire to the parlor upstairs."

Solomon waited until the crowd of guests had flooded out of sight and turned to Tanya. "It would be a shame to have to end the night so early. Would you like to join us in welcoming Mr. Sterling back to the party? Or would you rather return to your room?"

Tanya wiped her eyes with the excess sleeve of her pink sweater and studied the room around them for a moment. How plain and empty it was again. The plank door held no lock that she could see. "I could use a drink after that," she said, almost as if asking permission. "And you didn't bring supper tonight. You said I could choose and you broke your promise."

"So I did," Solomon nodded with an apologetic smile. "I've had a bit of a buffet prepared upstairs. And to show you that I'm a man of my word, as long as the rest of the night goes well, I will provide a banquet of your choosing for breakfast, complete with knife and fork if you wish."

Tanya looked again around the room, noting the totes were removed from the corner and a large splash of liquid had spread in the center of the floor. "Did...did you kill him?"

Solomon laughed just loud enough to echo. "Quite the opposite, Miss Johnston. I've shown him life like he's never known. I've freed his mind of the suffering of trying to survive this terrible world. Free from worry. From regret.

179

And with any luck, he will choose to stay and enjoy such a life rather than piss it away on existential struggles as many do."

"It sounds kind of like being on vacation without the trip."

"I knew you'd understand. You can't buy this level of serenity on a beach or aboard some cruise. While it is still, regrettably, temporary, its effects last much longer and leave us healthier and stronger for the investment."

She tried to hide the anger in her voice. "And you think I want this? That's why you wanted me to see?"

He began to lead her up the stairs. "You may not want it right now. But everyone does. And most will spend their entire lives toiling for even a sample of something similar, and usually aren't healthy or young enough by then to appreciate it. You're upset, and understandably so." Solomon offered her a patient smile. "But you will not only want it, but VIE for it in your own time. All you need do is search yourself with honest intentions. What we experience is the same as anyone on Earth has ever hoped, prayed, or wished for. And many claim to have achieved it. But we all know that's a lie based on sacrifice, concession, and weak comparison of unreachable horizons. They settle. They get used to it. They accept it and learn to love their version of the best they can manage in what's left of their health. And then they dry up inside with regret and pain and the routine of waiting for death."

Tanya fought the urge to run while only Solomon remained to stop her. Or was it her will to stay and hear more of his promises?

She shook her head with tightly closed eyes to find clarity and chose to press him further. "Isn't all that what makes being human special though? Playing against the clock? Having limits and testing them? Knowing that we don't have forever and to cherish what we've struggled for?"

Solomon chuckled again. "That's very romantic. It's also very depressing. If you think people enjoy planning for tomorrow only to find out their back hurts too much or they never make enough money or don't have the bodily autonomy to enjoy it to its fullest once you've earned it, then you've been sold the greatest lie in our society. The very essence of the cliché, 'Hook, line, and sinker.'"

Tanya fidgeted with her hands and bit her lip with a confused, squished brow. She asked carefully. "How... how long does it last? It's in the drink, isn't it? Is it like being drunk?"

"That's a fair assumption. And comparison. Though it doesn't depend on how big you are or how much you've eaten, or if you have a tolerance." Solomon looked and sounded only too happy to share his experience. He balled up his hands and closed his eyes like he was tasting it again for the first time. "The best way to describe it, is that the warmth of the drink takes over your whole body, inside and out. And it very slowly cools off." He finished with his palms flat, slowly moving down and letting out a long breath like a tantric release.

"I'm surprised you'd share all of this with a prisoner," Tanya dared.

Solomon stopped her at the top of the stairs and looked

proudly across the main hall to the commotion in the parlor. He returned his gaze to her with a confident, almost sympathetic smile. "Miss Johnston, there is not a single piece of information I could give you that you could use to harm me or these people. This knowledge is only powerful to those who give themselves to it. Those who take the chance to live as they never have before." He pulled a knife from his belt and flicked the blade out to pull across his palm. The cut was deep and bled immediately, trickling down his wrist as he made a tight fist again. He pulled a handkerchief from a pocket and wiped his hand to show the cloth stained with blood, but the cut had healed and left no scar. Then he cleaned the blade and sheathed it. "I feel you've earned that drink. Let's go see the new and improved Mr. Sterling."

"But he's-" Tanya caught a glimpse of a face outside the window that she recognized to be Mama as Solomon was walking her across to the parlor.

"Um, I don't think I need that drink anymore. I'm not sure my head can handle it just yet. I think I'd just like some air, if I could maybe take a walk outside, or at least open a window. I feel hot."

"Is that right? Well, there will be time for that, my guests are waiting. I insist. The testimony of rebirth is usually only witnessed by those who have already come alive."

Solomon offered his arm and patiently waited for her to take it. Tanya could no longer see Mama outside and blinked away her feeling of hope that warmed her cheeks. She cleared her throat and obliged Solomon by wrapping her fingers at his elbow. She flicked her hair back, ready to pretend a while longer, as he walked her to the parlor.

Sterling had his tie undone with a broad smile on his face as he pulled his pocket square to clean his glasses. "Hell, I'm not even sure I need these anymore!" He blinked several times through the lenses as he held them toward the light and then folded them into his breast pocket. "How is this possible?" He cracked his knuckles with a long stretch above his head and pushed his chin to one side until his neck gave an audible pop at which he sighed with such joy. "My god! I swear that's been stiff since my last high school football game!"

Solomon led Tanya into the parlor and left her near the door where Mr. Christian stepped in behind her. The vibrant host poured two drinks and brought them back to Tanya to clink his glass against hers.

"My friends," Solomon addressed the crowd who had mostly doffed their fezzes. "To new blood kindling with the old. To embracing the spirit. And to those who gave their very souls beneath these floors to preserve something worth believing. Salut!"

Tanya feigned a drink and looked sidelong over the crowd to see Mama peeking in the far window. She turned from the celebrating party and ran into Mr. Christian, spilling her caramel-colored drink across his pressed white shirt.

"I'm so sorry." She wiped her hand across his firm, barreled chest as if it would help. "I'm, um, not feeling well. That one sip is turning my stomach. I just need to get some air, I think.

Would you take me outside?"

Mr. Christian looked over toward Solomon and took a firm grasp of her wrist to stop her spreading the stain. "That's quite enough. If you don't wish to stay with us, I'll escort you back to your room."

Tanya attempted to yank back, making a loud fuss and pulling with everything she had. "Let go of me! I don't want to go to my room. I said I need some fucking air!" She made a show of trying to escape his hold on her and stole a look back to the window to see Mama duck out of sight.

Mr. Christian lost patience and smacked her face. He lifted her onto his shoulder while she kicked the air and pounded on his back. Her attempts to get free were half-hearted. She pretended to have exhausted herself and held her breath intermittently to build up the heat and color on her face as he carried her out of the room and up the stairs . When he reached the room, he put her down just inside on the floor and slammed the door shut.

She sat up after his key left the lock and she ran to the bathroom to start pulling again at the seashell sconce. She planted her foot high on the wall below the fixture and pulled and wiggled until the screws stripped and she fell to the floor with the decorative piece in her hands.

She pulled open the window and began chipping at the high slats until one broke and fell out. She stopped swinging long enough to scratch two words into the next one. MAMA HELP. She chipped the ends carefully until it fell from the window to the snow below.

Tanya closed the window and pulled the curtain to hide her work. She went back into the bathroom, huffing for breath, to see if she could return the sconce to the wall somehow. When she couldn't fix it, she chose to make the most of it and slammed the fixture into the mirror. Tanya selected a shard of glass suitable as a weapon and hid it under her mattress before returning to the door.

She took many deliberate swings at the door with the seashell sconce to cause noticeable damage to the wood. "They found me. I wasn't imagining, was I?" She shook her head hard to try to reassure herself. "If that wasn't Mama, you're really screwed, T. But it was. It had to be."

Chapter Twenty - Bad Moon on the Rise

"Wake up, baby. You gonna wanna see this."

Simon woke to the sound of Mama whispering in his ear. "Hmm? Look at what?"

Mama pointed toward the fireplace that still licked tiny flames over charred branches. Above the fire, hovering near the mantle, were two faintly glowing orbs bobbing together like they were warming themselves over conversation.

"I'm sure it must be our boys," Mama said. "Fisher's been gone since you nodded off. He run off and brought Mr. Joshua here. Somehow, even with this storm brewing and clouds blocking the sun, ever since they come, the house feels brighter and warmer."

"It sure does. I can almost smell your stew on the stove." Simon stood up and moved toward the orbs. He tried to touch them and stepped in between them. They weren't cold like he expected. His hands moved through them. He hung his head then. "Almost. I have to go back for Reno and Sam. Even if we stay here, this place won't feel like a home without them."

The orbs both moved away, then toward Mama, then disappeared out the door.

"Maybe that's just what Fisher came to hear you say. Look at them go!" Mama pulled the door open and changed form to chase them.

Simon wasted no time in following. Before long, they could see the edge of the golf course with its thinner snow on the broad fairways. Mama stopped and waited for Simon behind the lip of a deep bunker and they watched as the orbs flew toward the mansion. They were much harder to see in the open with the snowy background, but the wolves pursued as best they could.

When they cleared the treeline around a pond, they could see many cars parked beside the mansion. Then the orbs, presumed to be Fisher and Joshua, flickered a pink color before darting off toward the low end of the driveway. Mama let out a low whine and turned to run toward the cars.

Simon stopped behind a large black sedan and changed back. "We've seen this before. But why the hell would anyone throw a party with it snowing like this?" The white flakes were thick and dense, coating everything but the hot hood centers. The burning oil smell confirmed these cars had recently been parked. Another car was turning into the farthest end of the driveway with its windshield wipers working to keep off the falling snow. Behind it was a red-helmeted rider on a motorcycle. "Mama, keep an eye on the boys, I'll be right back."

As they split up, Simon changed to get closer to the car which was turning around in the narrow space of the paved lane. The biker had raised his visor to speak to the other driver and then drove up closer to the house. Simon recognized the biker as the man who put a knife in his back during his last encounter with Blake. Then, just before the car began to drive away, he could see Mo's face through the window. Simon ran ahead through the trees to get himself on the road before Mo could make the turn and became human again to stand upright and block the way.

The car came around and slid to a stop on the packed snow. Simon put his hands up facing the headlights and walked toward the car making sure he could be seen.

Mo rolled down his window. "Are you crazy running out on the road like this? Wait, Simon? The hell?"

Simon approached the window and crouched down. "I'm running low on patience and friends, so I'm only going to ask once. Are you part of this, friend?"
Gia leaned over Mo's lap toward Simon. "Tanya's in that house on the hill. I know she is! And we came up to check it out but big brother here won't let me go knock on the damn door!"

Simon put his hands out and shrugged. "Your brother is right. If you know she's in the house, what's she doing here?"

"Gia, sit down." When she didn't move, Mo pounded the steering wheel. "I said sit the fuck down! Damn! We just laid all this out with Blake, and he had us followed up here by his biker buddy. Tanya's mixed up with this new crowd. Might be dating one of them. But Gia and Blake have reason to believe they're nothing but trouble."

"Blake is right. Make sure you tell him I said so." Simon warmed his arms as he spun to look up and down the road. Heavy snow blew into the car window.

"You ain't got a coat out here?" Gia asked. "Why are you up here?"

"I'll have to catch up with you on that later. I just know these assholes are bad news, and I've been waiting for a sign that Tanya isn't in on it."

"My girl isn't-"

Simon cut Gia short. "Money can change people. But like I said, I need to be sure. She hasn't left the house since their first party a couple of nights ago. And now they're having another one. Must be in a back room or something though, I can't see anything going on."

"Does that mean you're going in after her?" Mo asked.

"It's complicated. If things get out of hand, someone could get hurt."

The sound of a motorcycle approaching had them all looking up the lane. At the same time, Mama ran up behind Simon and stopped to catch her breath.

"Simon! I got something you need to see." Mama handed Simon a small piece of wood with two words scratched into it.

Simon handed the piece over to Mo and stood up, looking at

the biker who came to a stop. "Get yourselves out of here. I'm not sure what we're going to do yet, but get this message to Blake. Tell him it's from Tanya."

Mama came closer. "I saw her. She was fighting to get free. And Sam and Reno are locked up in that shelter outside. We can't open it, baby. But I heard them in there slamming around. They're okay. They know we're here."

"How'd you get past the cameras?" Mo asked.

Simon narrowed his eyes, "You saw the cameras from the end of the lane?"

Mo closed his eyes a moment, realizing he had let it slip out. "I know some things about the place. I can explain later. If you need to get by them again, the power supply should be easy enough to cut off from the outside. Or even cut a line from the pole out here."

"So, what? That's it? You got all this help and we're leaving?" Gia asked.

Deacon revved his bike and put his hands out impatiently.

"You can't be here if something goes down. Besides, we're outnumbered and knee-deep in our own shit. If you can think of a way to round up a posse or something, we might have a chance at controlling the outcome." Simon shifted his weight and gave a nod to Mama, who was skulking in some dead brush opposite him from the car. She quickly ran off toward the house. "We're watching for the right time to make a move. Go get out of this weather, be safe, and make sure you tell Blake what I said."

Simon turned to follow Mama but looked back to see that Mo and the biker following them had gotten on their way.

Mama gave Simon a concerned look when he caught up to her. "New friends of yours? Do you think they're smart enough to stay away?"

"I doubt they'd do anything stupid. That guy driving the car knows about us. Long story. He's smart, though. He'll stay away."

"What about your brother?"

"He's in a mess of his own. Probably why he sent his biker buddy." Simon shook his head with a look to the sky as a gust of snow flew at them when the wind changed direction. "I just wanted to let him know that I have an eye on Tanya. We don't need any more complications. We've waited long enough."

Mama rounded on him and blocked his path. "There's something else you're not telling me. I can feel it. As soon as I told you that girl needed help, the Simon I knew would have torn that place apart to get to her. Especially with your friends leaving none the wiser about us being here. What's wrong, baby?"

Simon dropped his chin. He tried to look anywhere except Mama's face, but knew she wouldn't have it. "She's in there.

Tanya's sister. The one she's been looking for. And she's the reason that asshole has Sam and Reno. I saw her stop them. Saw them drop to the floor in front of her." Simon pushed both hands through his wet hair to get it out of his face. "And after what Fisher said about putting the pack first, I-"

"You told us you didn't know how it happened!" Mama scolded him. "You know good and damn well that when my boys lie, it makes Mama crazy."

"I wasn't lying. I don't know. I've never seen anything like it. I was frozen in my tracks when it happened. I couldn't make sense of it. And I'm..." Simon couldn't keep looking at her. He searched the sky for the moon again, unable to see it for the bluster of snow and the heavy clouds. "I'm afraid I'll lose you all if I charge in and lose control."

"There's something you told me a long, long time ago, that I ain't never gonna forget." Mama took hold of his chin and pulled his face to meet her eyes. "You gotta trust your gut when your head gets in the way. And if we fall when we try to do the right thing, it's just one less monster in the world that might hurt somebody we love. You remember saying those words to me when I stood over the pieces of my husband?"

Simon tried to pull back but she held on. "I remember. You'd just lost Luther. You were out of control and you wanted me to stop you from doing something to yourself."

"I BEGGED you to strike me down!" Her lip trembled with a mixture of anger and sadness. "I even tried to provoke you. As I recall, your first meeting with Reno wasn't too different. And both times you let us come around on our own. Gave us time to make our own choice. You showed us a way when we ain't even want one! You just pressed on and did what YOU knew to be right. Because that's what it takes to keep a family moving forward instead of looking back."

She let go of his chin and placed her cold hands on either side of his face. His cheeks were burning hot with conflicted feelings.

"My gut says we don't understand what we're up against. And that what Joshua said doesn't make sense. Not yet." Simon repeated the words Mama told him. "We can't see in the storm for the eye. Drowning in spirit."

"And shifting current. It's gettin' all jumbled up now."

"Joshua… This spirit of Joshua spoke in circles when I met him, too." Simon touched her shoulder to turn her around so they could keep moving. "Maybe if he said it backwards, there might be something useful if we turn it the other way?"

"Baby, I love my Joshua. But he been alone in a different world for years." Mama pointed toward the house as it came back into view. "I thought you should also know about those vehicles. See 'em there? Parked up next to that storm room or whatever the hell it is. Like they gonna try to race each other across the field or something."

The wind blew at them again and Simon held Mama's arm. "Shifting current. The storm is moving. Shifting. We can't see Luna watching."

"Yeah, I bet those cameras can't see nothing, either."

They exchanged a look and changed back into wolf form to make a run back up to the house. When they reached the hedge where they had been hidden before, they could see the same camera whose tiny red activation light flickered on and off with the drifting snow. They took their time snooping around the vehicles Mama pointed out. There were four matched, soft-top covered Jeeps, two of each were parked on either side of the shelter. Simon watched the camera to be sure he wouldn't be spotted and changed to use his hands so he could pull the snaps and crawl into the back of one.

Inside the snug space was a rack of assault rifles and the floor was lined with red plastic cases. Simon flipped open a case to find rows of loaded magazines to fit the rifles. He looked back through the vinyl window for the camera and slipped out with two ammo boxes. He made his way carefully back to Mama and opened a box.

"They're planning a hunt. Look at these." Simon pulled a magazine and started pushing out the cartridges into the snow. "I don't know about going in, but when they come out, they're going to get a surprise. Leave two in each mag and put them back in the case. If they're going to set Sam and Reno loose, they'll get a couple of shots and think the guns are jammed. It'll buy us the time we need to turn things around."

Mama shot Simon a look of disbelief and set to work unloading and covering the discards with snow. He returned with two more when Mama had just finished the first magazine.

"How many more?"

Simon caught his breath and popped the lids. "Four cases in the first Jeep. I'm guessing they'll all be the same. I'll help with these before I go back for more."

"Why not just take the guns?"

"I don't want them to suspect anything and call off opening that shelter. When we're done with these, I want you to slip up there like you did before and tell Reno what's going on so he and Sam can lead the jeeps out. And then I'll track down Fisher so we can start snooping out how many problems we'll have left inside the house when they start their fun."

Chapter Twenty-One - Unlock and Load

Blake used his foot to push a towel around the floor where the others had tracked wet footprints into his apartment. A knock on the door made his eyes roll and he lay the towel out flat before answering.

Agent Waites leaned against the doorframe with an expectant look. "Are you going to invite me in?"

"If you needed an invitation, you wouldn't be here. Wipe your feet." Blake walked away toward his futon and grabbed the ashtray to dump in the trash. He lit a cigarette and returned to sit.

Agent Waites closed the door slowly and stood on the ratty towel looking at Blake's apartment interior. "You've been here for a few years and have nothing on your walls. No pictures of family or friends, or even your bike. A yard sale television that must be at least twenty years old. Is it even a color set?"

"This isn't home. It never was, and it never will be. It's temporary." Blake took a long drag and finally looked up at Waites who had her hair down. It was much longer than he remembered, or maybe it had always been pinned or tied. "Is this a social call? As you can see, I'm rather busy on one of my very few days off."

"You smoke a lot, too. That can't be good for your health."

"I'd have a drink too, but it's too expensive. Gotta pick your poison." Blake propped his feet up and threw an arm up over the back of the futon. "What's yours, Miss Waites? Margaritas? Maybe some 'medicinal' marijuana to relax you while going over files? Men?"

She smoothed her heavy black hair behind one ear. "I don't think I'd care to discuss that."

"Women, then? Hey, I'm not one to judge. Just making conversation until you get to the point."

Agent Waites took a long breath and pulled the chair from the kitchen table to sit in front of the small TV. "The point is I still don't have a warrant, my partner hasn't reported in, and I need some help."

"I think you're asking the wrong person," Blake deflected. "In case you forgot, I have my own problems." He wiggled his foot until his pant leg rode up and revealed the ankle monitor.

"You didn't let me finish. I can help you if you agree to help me. It's not as big an ask as you might think it is. I just need to know if Agent Sterling is okay. You're pretty cunning when you get a chance, and I'm hoping you can get our suspect to let you in to use a bathroom or a phone or something and snoop around a minute. And I'd give you free rein to defend yourself if there's any kind of struggle."

"Defend myself? You're going to give me a gun?" Blake grinned as he sat up and crushed out his cigarette. "I've been a good boy. I've followed the rules. And now it sounds like you're tempting me to break them and dig my hole deeper. There are a few problems I have with your favor. First, you haven't offered me anything. You said you could help me, but I'm sure you don't have anything I want."

"I think I do. My boss is pretty keen to protect his agents." Waites stared hard at Blake for any reaction. "He gave me the go-ahead to unfreeze your assets and agreed that you are no longer within the statute for probation on the crime for which you've been accused. So the monitor can come off too, unless you have some reason to continue living this way. You'll still have to meet your court date, of course, if they ever set one. I've even found you an attorney in case you haven't made any calls since I suggested it."

Blake stared back at her, bored. He leaned on his knees and gave his full attention as if he'd just been scolded for nodding off in high school. "I told you I'm fine with my attorney."

"I'm not asking. It's already in order. You can call your guy and let him know, or he can find out when he gets his walking papers from my office." Waites took a deep breath and folded her hands. "She's good. She owes me a pro bono case and yours is good for her, as long as everything you've said so far is true. All they want is your case in the news since there's such a big claim on the line. She says it'll be good press for the insurance company she represents, as it happens to be the same one holding the claim for Blush when it was burned."

Blake picked up his pack, jostled his last two cigarettes, and popped one up to his lips. He tossed the pack on the table and lit his smoke, savoring the first long drag as the end flared with a flash of fire.

"That's a lot of strings you pulled for me to just go play dumb for this playboy of yours. If he's got your friend, I want a gun and I want permission to use it." Blake kept his gaze fixed on his cigarette as he rolled it between his fingers and watched it smolder. "I want Gordy off my back, too. If that sack of shit so much as adjusts his little cap in my direction, he's gonna need a lot of backup to stop me from dragging him by his crooked badge into a dark alley. Promote him, demote him, transfer him. Whatever. That guy has been busting my balls ever since I got this damn bracelet and I've had enough."

"I'll see what I can do about that. I'm sure I can put a word in with Internal Affairs. Chief Poffo is planning to overhaul the department now that midterms are through." Waites reached for her belt and placed a stun gun on the table. "It's mine, not a department issue. I'll get another one, or you can return it. I don't care which. Does this mean I can count on you for some answers?"

Blake's phone bleated and vibrated across the uneven table. He scooped it up to answer when he saw Mo's number on the screen. "Yeah?" Blake stood and stretched and paced the short distance to the kitchen and back. He responded with a few agreeable hums to keep the call private from Agent Waites as Mo told him about his findings at the country club mansion.

When Mo started talking, Blake adjusted the volume on his phone to keep the words from carrying. "Listen B, I didn't see much. Your boy, uh, Deacon, took a quick ride around the place and said there was a party going on. Lots of cars. Maybe twenty or so. But the main floor was dark and he couldn't see in. Got a look at some little bald guy out walking in the snow with no coat on. Maybe he was drunk or something, stumbling around. You got company or something?"

"Uh-huh. I hear you."

"Snow slowed down a bit but is still laying, so I'm gonna run Gia home and get back to your place."

Gia hollered over Mo. Blake had to yank the phone away from his ear. "Like hell I'ma go home! Simon gave you a message and I know it's from Tanya. You think I don't recognize him? I'm with you 'til I get some answers!"

Blake cleared his throat as he continued pacing. "You called me to listen to you fight?"

Mo came back quickly, "Yeah, my bad. Simon stopped us on the way out, said he's watching the house and we should bounce. We're a couple of minutes away from your place."

Blake laughed, "He's right about that. I'll be here." Blake ended the call and went back to Agent Waites and put his foot up on the table. "So whether or not I get what you want, you can show me some faith by getting this thing off of me."

Agent Waites reluctantly nodded, "I guess I'll have to if I'm going to trust you. Was that your biker friend?"

"That was none of your business," Blake huffed impatiently. "But I'm about to have company, so I'd appreciate it if we could get this over with before the place gets too crowded."

Waites bent to her knees on the floor in front of him. "You really should quit smoking, especially in this place. Even in your shape, a guy your age needs to consider his health." She fumbled in her pocket for a key fob device and pulled her hair out of her face to one side. She had just removed the ankle monitor when the door burst open.

Deacon entered and stared a moment. A smile stretched the corners of his mouth and he stuck his tongue out as Blake casually adjusted the waistband of his sweatpants. "Guilty or not, that's hot enough for me." He playfully fanned his face with his gloves.

Gia pushed in past DX and looked at Blake in shock. "Who the hell is this bitch?"

"I guess I should have been quicker." Waites stood up and flipped her hair back with a sigh. "I thought you said I had a few minutes." She turned toward the door to walk out as Mo entered the apartment. "It's nothing personal, just business. Excuse me."

When Mo saw Gia reach for her earrings, he lunged in to grab her by the waist and held her against the counter as she flailed and shouted in Spanish.

Deacon gestured to the door like a game show host and couldn't contain his laughter. "You better go fast. The storm outside ain't nothing compared to what you just started."

Agent Waites strode out the door. Deacon closed it and stood guard in front of it.

When Mo let go, Gia challenged Deacon to get out of the way. "Move or I'll move you, asshole!"

Deacon looked down at her and crossed his arms. He nodded toward Blake who had just stamped out his cigarette.

Blake went to the closet, pushed aside a couple of hanging garments, and pulled a panel out of the ceiling to hand to Gia who had cornered him there.

Gia threw down the panel and confronted him. "You just gonna ignore what I saw?"

Blake pulled himself up into the space he had made and entered the tiny crawl space. He grabbed a rucksack and pushed it through the opening. "Look out!" The heavy bag hit the floor at Gia's feet and he crawled his way back out with a bounce in front of her.

"I'll have to explain later, we have shit to do." Blake tossed the rucksack on the futon with a muffled, heavy thud. "Deac, if you want to dig in on this, I'd appreciate it. Mo, you said you got a look at some of those cameras. Do we have a line on them?"

Mo looked confused. "Uh, yeah. But I can't just tap it from anywhere. I have some gear at my place that'll work. But it'll take a few minutes to get set."

Deacon moved to the futon and opened the bag. "Oh, ho! Here we go! You've been holding out on me, man! Are we rolling up or rolling out?"

"Probably both," Blake answered and then turned to Mo. "Uh, your place is no good. Stairs and all that. Besides, I need to grab something from the garage. Can you grab your stuff and meet us there to hook up?"

Gia stood between the men and put her hands out. "No! Stop! Ain't nobody leaving this room until you tell me what I need to know! Who was that woman, and what the hell do you need a shotgun for?"

Deacon had pulled a short 12-gauge from the bag and began loading it. "Is this one for me, bro?"

"Not a chance. That's my good luck charm. But you can have that stun gun over there."

Gia got close to Mo and demanded he explain. "Gilly, what gear are you talking about? What are you guys doing?" She rounded on Blake again as he pulled some jeans and shirts from his closet. "Whatever it is, you can't. You just can't! You're on probation! You ain't about to roll up on nobody with a damn shotgun!"

Blake took off his pants as both men groaned playfully. He revealed the marks on his ankle where the bracelet had been removed. "An hour ago, you wanted me to do something

203

about your friend that you thought nobody but you cared about. Now you don't want me to go? Is being with you going to be like this all the time, or is this a special occasion?" He pulled on jeans and fastened chaps into place before rolling on socks and grabbing his boots.

"Being with me?" Gia was dumbfounded. "When did we get to you being with me? I've never seen you like this. Is this the real you?"

Blake pushed his arms into flannel sleeves and stepped close to her. "This is as real as it gets." He leaned down and kissed her for the first time. He pulled her against him and held her longer than he should until she stopped slapping at his arms. When he broke the kiss, he looked into her amber eyes. "She's not just your friend. If this isn't what you want, I get it. But I'm going." He let go and walked away before she could react and grabbed his rucksack to leave. "Mount up, Regulator."

Deacon bumped his fist against Blake's and followed him out the door without closing it. "You can see yourselves out, right?"

Gia ran out into the hall after them and shouted from the doorway, "You better not think about kissing me again with that smoke on your breath!"

Chapter Twenty-Two - Bound and Determined

Tanya grew tired of defacing her bedroom door and fetched the shard of broken glass from her mattress. Melissa's voice came to her again, now with a desperate, throaty echo. She could no longer make out words even though it sounded closer than before. A terrible combination of cries and pleas overlapped until Tanya was almost dizzy from trying to focus with her eyes squeezed shut.

Tanya went to sit on the floor with a fixed stare through the keyhole. The chandelier in the main hall gave just enough light to the staircase that she could see across to the other door where she was taken to see Melissa. The memory of seeing her sister unmoving on the bed made her rub at the sore spot on her shoulder again.

Missy's voice faded into silence. The lonely quiet left Tanya with fidgeting hands and watery eyes. She closed her eyes again and tried to imagine the sight of Melissa in the bed across the balcony.

"I wish you could hear me, too. I'm so close. I don't know how to help you. I don't even know how to help myself."

She tried to see through the keyhole again and caught sight of a shadow on the stairs. When the barrel-chested Mr. Christian turned toward Tanya, she swatted the light switch off. Tanya moved behind where the door would swing inward and clutched her makeshift weapon. Her heart pounded so fast that it made her squeeze her hands too tight and the glass cut into the skin just enough to make her bite her tongue.

The key turned quickly and the door pushed open. Mr. Christian didn't enter. Tanya watched as the head of his shadow leaned and turned to look for her in the rectangular patch of light on the floor.

"Miss Johnston, show yourself. I've brought you a little surprise from our party. Mr. Solomon has had a change of heart and would like you to join us." He took a step inside and reached for the light switch.

Tanya took a chance and shoved the door with every bit of strength she could muster. It slammed into Mr. Christian and she took a swipe at his exposed wrist. The shard broke against the wall during her swing and made the piece smaller and cut deeper into her palm.

He threw his weight into the heavy wood and sent Tanya sprawling to the floor. "I'm glad to see you're feeling better. It'll make tonight more fun for our guests."

When she turned to stand up, she saw a length of chain draped around the man's shoulder and he began to pull it free with a heavy clank on the hardwood floor. Mr. Christian wrapped one end of the chain around his hand and curled it into a fist. Attached to the last link in his hand, he held a metal tent spike with its sharp point exposed.

"I'd much rather you come along willingly. But if you want to try me, I'd be happy to have some of my own fun." He smiled at her with narrowed eyes and his crooked bottom teeth showing.

Tanya lunged forward and ducked under his arm when he swung at her. She stumbled and nearly lost her footing. She dropped the broken mirror shard, scrambling to her feet just as something hard and heavy struck her between the shoulders. Her hands flew up instinctively to catch herself from hitting her face when she fell. She felt herself scream but couldn't hear it. Her breath was knocked out of her chest. Tanya stretched her arms to pull herself forward when Mr. Christian stepped on the middle of her back.

She watched helplessly as his shadow on the wall pulled a small hoop from his pocket. Then he dropped part of it and she recognized a pair of handcuffs. The brute bent down and pulled one of her arms behind her back so hard that her shoulder audibly popped. When her scream came out this time, he grabbed a fistful of her hair and pressed her face into the carpet to muffle the sound. He slapped a cuff onto her wrist and linked the other into the eye of a chain link. He rolled her body over twice until her arms were pinned to her sides like a human spool.

Mr. Christian gathered a meaty handful of the chains to lift her up by the waist. Her stomach lurched from the sudden forced motion and she spat vomit down his back when her belly struck his shoulder. He stopped suddenly and turned toward the closed door where Melissa lay behind it on the bed.

Tanya gurgled and sputtered to breathe. A cacophonous

shriek that sounded like Melissa echoed in her aching head. While Mr. Christian stood still, Tanya kicked her legs and felt herself breaking free from her perch. The brute lowered his arm to let her go and lumbered toward the closed door. Tanya dropped awkwardly to the top step and began to tumble down the stairs with the chain unwinding. The chandelier light spun in and out of sight until her head struck the thick, solid newel post. The twinkling crystal faces that hung high above her dulled and disappeared.

***

The face of Mr. Christian with his prominent chin loomed clearly in sight, but no matter how Melissa scratched and climbed toward it, it hung just out of reach. She clung with bleeding fingertips and split nails to a billowing satin cloth. The listless face glowed a dull blue like a slowly suffocating moon bearing the man's features, with no sign of being attached to the man's body.

"Come closer," Melissa ordered. "I can't reach."

The cloth shredded under her sharp nails and she slid down. Melissa caught a binding cord at the bottom and clutched tightly to hold on. She looked down and saw herself far below, pinned to a four-poster bed. The body stretched out where she could see the hands and feet of her other self were punctured by the thin, sharp tip of each post.

A broad door near the bed thumped over and over. Something or someone on the other side was determined to get through. Melissa began to swing back and forth, aiming for the door. The torn cloth broke away before she could get the angle right and she plummeted head over heels toward her splayed body below. She couldn't tell if she was shrinking or her other self was growing. She righted herself in the fall until she could dive toward the chest.

She expected a collision but instead continued to fall into a vast, rib-lined cavity that swelled with boiling heat. A sudden and terrible stop pulled at her ankles. She was suspended only an arm's length above a boiling silvery liquid. As she hung and slowly spun, a swelling bubble of thin, reflective, liquid metal grew close to her. She tucked her arms up and tried to bend to reach whatever had bound her ankles. The bubble touched her dangling hair and became a molten weight that pulled harder.

She reached her ankles and climbed hand over hand until she was upright and staring up at the face again. His resting expression blocked the opening she fell through. Melissa's hair fell across her back, searing her flesh and nearly causing her to fall. She tensed all over her body and tried to force any number of her known vampiric advantages to come back to her. Her shoulder blades burned and stretched until leathery wings pushed out through the ruined flesh and began to carry her upward.

The glowing face became brighter and larger as Melissa flew closer until the giant mouth above seemed just within reach.

"Open!" she shrieked. When the man's lips parted, that same broad door was revealed behind his lips. "Open the door!"

Unable to stop her momentum, she slammed into the wood and landed on the inside of his teeth. When her feet touched down, the wings she had just learned to fly with ripped away and fell below into the boiling silver lake. Across the gap of parted teeth stood the shadow man she had seen before. He reached up into the keyhole of the door and twisted his arm. Melissa started to speak when the shadow man was pulled up through the keyhole and vanished from sight. She leaped the gap to the other side as the mouth opened. She could barely grab hold to keep from falling and found herself dangling again as the mouth began to close. The teeth she held onto narrowed and sharpened.

She looked up to the hand-sized keyhole and demanded, "The key! I need the key!"

Melissa pulled herself up between the teeth as the blue moon mouth started to close. Sweltering darkness crept around her. She reached up toward the keyhole and the last sliver of light revealed an eye staring back through. With the mouth now closed, she reached up to push her hand into the opening as the shadow man had before her. With a twist that clicked a mechanism, her hand was stuck. The toothy foothold beneath her had become too narrow and she felt the keyhole clamp around her wrist, cutting into the skin.

Melissa hung in the dark. In the consuming silence.

Chapter Twenty-Three - Tooth and Nail

Simon and Mama sneaked out of sight from the Jeeps just before the party guests poured out to start the engines. From a space behind the driveway hedges, Simon couldn't see how many people had piled into the vehicles. Mama pointed to a large man carrying a blonde woman out into the drifting snow toward a flat part of the golf course. Simon snarled but held his ground. The wait was agonizing until they saw the large man returning alone.

Mama squeezed his arm. "I know you've been patient. But we can't go off now. When they open the doors, I'll run for our girl. You chase down Reno and make sure we're playing the same game here."

"What the hell is that supposed to mean?"

Mama gave Simon a wide-eyed, admonishing stare. "You know better than anybody what started this mess. He's unhinged sometimes. For all we know, when they open that door, he and Sam just gonna start tearing into each other again. You gotta make sure we all on the same page before you turn to take on these animals."

Simon smirked at her use of the word and nodded.

"It's only a little smile, but I'll take it, baby. I'ma start creeping down closer to get a head start, just in case I need some wiggle room. You be careful, now." Mama nudged against his arm playfully and hid her worry so he wouldn't see. She turned to move down the hill around the far end of the driveway.

As the sun sank, Simon could hear a man speaking and the voice drew his eyes to a second-story balcony where large spotlights were being fixed into place. The lights flicked on and turned to face the direction Tanya had been carried.

The voice from the balcony shouted into the wind. "My friends, we share a drink to gather our spirits! Happy hunting!"

Simon could see only the hands of a few people extending glasses from the balcony edge, but the lights did not allow him to see faces. The snow seemed to stop falling abruptly as if reacting to the announcement, but the wind picked up with a jarring chill.

The Jeep engines starting almost drowned out the sound of heavy metallic banging, followed by familiar growls. The vehicles each drove out in turn. As Simon watched, the passengers tore off the softer covers and threw them away so they could stand in the moving vehicles with their rifle barrels pointing upward or outward. Excited shouts and whistles sounded off from the passengers as the Jeeps drove around the parking area and waited far away from the house, pointing their headlights where the balcony spotlights shone.

Simon heard gunfire from the balcony that set things into motion. The two beasts he recognized as Sam and Reno leaped out from the shelter that held them and down the hill toward the parking lot. He watched as they ran across the tops of the cars parked there, denting in roofs and smashing headlights and windshield glass.

He took one last look at the sky, finally able to faintly see the moonlight behind dark, thick clouds. It was full and seemed immense with its bluish glow. Simon bolted upright and succumbed to the large hulking beast form he seldom called upon while mouthing a wish that Luna would guide him.

***

Tanya woke with a start to face a black wolf pulling on her chain. "Mama?"

She held her head from the throbbing pain. The wolf whined and led her to the end of her chain spiked into the ground. The hair on the wolf's back and face receded until Tanya could see Mama crouched at the spike just as she yanked it loose with an exerted grunt.

"Come on, Angel, we got to go, NOW!"

Mama reached out for her hand and Tanya took it. The women ran away from the house until they reached a bunker to dive into. Just as they got low into the snowy sand, two large beasts leaped overhead and turned to face the women with snapping, drooling teeth bared.

"Run, baby! Run, I say!"

Tanya felt frozen in fear where she cowered and saw Mama

grow into something that matched these nightmarish hulks in front of her. She had managed to turn her head and crawl up the lip of the sandy pit when another beast lunged over her head toward the other three. Snapping and snarling could be heard as she covered her head and face and screamed into her arms. A short series of gunshots rang out and when she looked up, the pack of werewolves had split off and out of sight.

The sound of a crash drew her attention to look over the bunker's lip again, but a gust of drifting snow whipped across her face. When she opened her eyes, another wolf stood at her feet in the bunker. The wolf quickly morphed into a tall, lanky man with curly hair hanging over one eye and he grinned at her.

"Trust me, you don't want to look," Fisher assured her. "Looks like I'm a little late. I gotta get in there, but let's get you away from here first."

"No, I can't! I have to go back. Missy is in that house!"

Fisher shook his head. "You gotta come with me, now. It's too dangerous up there."

Tanya pulled her arm away when Fisher reached for her. "If you're not going to help me get in, then go help the others. There's a tunnel somewhere that leads back into the house and I'm going in to get my sister. I just don't have the key to her door."

Fisher blew a cloud of steam and looked around as another

heavy crash and gunshots sounded. "I've seen the tunnel. Come on, quick!"

Fisher changed again to a wolf and waited for her to coil up the chain cuffed to her wrist, throw a leg over his back, and grab his neck fur to start their run to the cellar tunnel.

***

"Are you sure you know what you're doing, B?" Mo asked as he sat at the desk at Whiskey Throttle with his laptop and a headset wrapped around his neck.

Blake watched the laptop screen as it showed the image captured by the camera attached to Deacon's helmet.

"Little man's got a point, bro." Deacon took the helmet and put it on. He fixed his belt, which held two handguns, and checked the shoulder harness under his jacket that held extra clips before zipping up. "We could use a plan."

Blake set his jaw and handed Deacon a backpack. "We don't have time to plan. Besides, the beauty of improvisation is that not having a plan never gets in the way of possibility." He pulled on a backpack of his own and threw a leg over one of the dirt bikes parked inside the garage. "That doesn't mean I'm not prepared."

He pulled the strap on his shoulder holster that held his short-barreled shotgun so it hid under his jacket and fastened a belt with a knife and a handgun.

"So we're just gonna ride up and raise hell?"

"Not exactly. We need some backup. But there's only time to make one call." Blake reached for his friend's helmet and pulled the bent microphone down from the ear clip headset closer to Deacon's mouth. "I got a little surprise for our pal, Officer Gordy. Mo, when we get out the gate, turn up my scanner I pulled from the closet. When you hear the reckless driver code 505, call up Waites to tell her it's me. Whether or not she can use that information, those cops chasing us are going to be the only backup we have on such short notice."

"You're asking a lot for somebody with no plan," Mo teased. "If your cell loses signal up there and the call drops, what should I do?"

"If you lose us, pack up your shit and go home. Don't get tempted to do anything stupid." Blake fixed his helmet cam, put it on, and tightened his chin strap. "You get a fix on the house cameras yet?"

Mo shook his head. "Not yet, might not get them to come up at all, since it's a newly installed system. I'll keep working at it though."

Deacon mounted the other bike and looked over at his own. "You know I don't like riding someone else's bike. And what the hell is in this pack? It's heavy."

Blake winked at him. "Roadside emergency kit." He flipped his visor down, started his bike, and then hit the wall switch to open the garage.

A mound of drifted snow had built up in the opening below the automatic door. As the two riders drove out, Deacon's back tire slipped sideways just enough to make him shout across the microphone.

Gia could be heard in the background over Blake's earpiece which served as a secondary sound check. "What can I do, Gilly? I can't just stand here and watch!"

Blake grinned to himself as he pointed for Deacon to split off. "Go make some noise and meet me on the road to the country club. I'll need you to show me which house it is. Hey, Mo. Tell Gia that some hot coffee and some sandwiches would be nice when we get back. There's a little bagel shop across the street closing soon if she doesn't want to be your extra eyes."

The bikers took opposite directions on the main street. Blake passed a plow truck flinging salt and spotted a police patrol car turning the corner ahead of him. He recognized the car number. "Gotcha, Gordy!"

He rode up on the car just as it stopped at a red light. Blake cranked the throttle and passed the car into the intersection. He whipped the rear wheel into a slide to circle donuts in the middle of the stopped traffic as car horns sounded. When the patrol car's blue and red bar lights flipped on, Blake peeled out to look for another.

Blake laughed out loud, "Got one already, buddy. How we doing?"

Deac's voice came back. "That was fast, dude. I'm rolling up on one now."

"Both hands on your grips, Deac. No guns til we get where we're going."

"Got it, bro. Guns ain't as fun as ridin' on the run. Here we go!"

Mo chimed in, "There's the code. Making the call now. Gia, watch these a minute."

Blake tore down the main drag toward the outskirts with the sirens bleating behind him. The sun was dipping out of sight under an overcast sky and the streetlights were flipping on as if guiding the way.

"Hey Deac, I think we're good to head up. How long to get there?"

Deacon's voice came back. "At this pace, we can do it in ten. But once we're off the city streets, it may be slick. Better figure on fifteen. I'm headed to the bridge."

Buildings blurred by as Blake sped through another intersection, nearly hitting a man in an overcoat crossing the street with his fist in the air. A patrol car with its bright lights strobing up ahead squealed to a stop sideways to try to block the road, but Blake swerved over to the sidewalk until it was clear to get back on the road.

"Yo, you know these bikes are running almost empty, right?"

"Don't worry, Deac. We only need them for a one-way trip."

"What the hell is that supposed to mean, man?" Deacon's voice sounded concerned.

"No worries. For evidence purposes, the owners went on a joy ride up to the country club and had an accident. The second reason I didn't want to take our bikes." Blake slowed as he approached the bridge until he saw the single headlight he was looking for.

"I see you, bro." Deacon almost came to a stop to be sure of the turn. They crossed the bridge in tandem and when they reached the other side, with at least four patrol cars in their rear view, he asked, "What's the first reason?"

"I didn't want to hear you whine about your bike getting scuffed again," Blake laughed.

Chapter Twenty-Four - Crux to Bear

Simon slammed into Reno and then turned to run back toward the gunner Jeeps. Reno showed no sign of slowing as he pursued. Simon couldn't be sure and dove out of the way of an oncoming Jeep. He looked back in time to see Reno throw himself at the vehicle, smash in the hood, and continue toward Simon.

There was no time to wait, so he baited Reno toward the mansion on the hill. Gunfire from the spotlit balcony rained down toward them once they had reached the parking lot. Simon caught a bullet in the shoulder and pushed forward to tear through the plastic curtain. Inside the house for the first time, he changed back to get a look around. He took hold of himself before the beast within could rule him and hid where he could see out the window.

To the sound of more gunshots and screams, he watched Reno leap to the balcony and send two men in overcoats flying from the second floor down into the snow. One of the spotlights fell to the patio below and shattered.

Simon turned from the window to find the large man that earlier carried Tanya was watching him with a rifle fixed on him.

"We had a feeling there would be more. What took you so long?" He pointed the gun barrel from his hip as Simon ran along the wall toward the open lounge doors.

Bullets followed his path and two hit him in the back as Simon rolled into the room. He threw a heavy chair at the window on the far side of the room and stood sideways behind the protruding brick of the fireplace. More shots rang out, spraying the room before the man would enter. When Simon heard a click and what he thought was an empty magazine hit the floor, he jumped out from his hiding place. Simon ran at the man and lunged, only to catch the butt stock of the gun in the back of his head as the man sidestepped him. He rolled Simon over and began taking heavy swings at Simon's face, bloodying his nose and mouth to the man's satisfaction.

When Simon didn't move or retaliate, the man stepped over him and reloaded his rifle, moving toward the front doors in the main hall. Simon took the opportunity, under cover of the gun reload sounds click-clacking into place, to roll to his feet and duck out through the plastic curtain. As Simon skulked around the outside of the building, unaware of Reno's location, he packed a handful of snow against his face to wipe away the blood and add cold pressure. He flung away the red snow and made his way to the front doors to recollect himself with a shake of his head.

His head pounded and his hunger felt heavy, urging him to embrace the change again. With a heavy breath, he felt an immense weight crash down on him from behind and another spray of gunfire came from within the house. As Simon rolled to his back, a torrent of bullets broke and zipped through the window above him into Reno, who turned to leap inside. The gunfire ceased from the first floor while another series of shots again came from the balcony, shooting toward where the remaining spotlight pointed.

Another loud crash of glass led Simon's eyes to his unhinged friend breaking through a faraway window just in time to slam into the side of an approaching Jeep. It was sent rolling down the steep part of the hill into the parking lot. One of the passengers was thrown out and Reno opened his jaws wide and tore part of the body away before trampling the rest of it on the way toward the rolling Jeep. When Simon looked back in through the nearby window, the large man had picked himself up and went to fetch his gun from the floor. He had four long, bloody claw marks down his back, reminding Simon of Reno's missing digit, and yet the man moved as if he were no worse off than when he had pummeled Simon only minutes before.

"What the hell?"

As Simon watched, the man pulled a flask from his pocket and slugged its contents down before flinging the decanter away. Simon's eyes went wide, but he was distracted again by the sight of Sam and Mama far off, crushing a Jeep between them with a sickening crunch of metal and cries of pain. Reno was barreling toward them but they baited him away, out of sight around the house.

Simon kept low and rolled himself down the snowy hill in case the cameras were watching or the man inside had come to look out the window. He was in a blind spot for himself and closed his eyes tightly to listen. He could hear footsteps inside the house gathering and, just after, from the driveway side of him, he could hear sirens approaching.

He crept farther from the house down into the parked and demolished cars that provided fair cover. He could see up to the balcony, which appeared to be empty but for the one remaining light. The three passengers who were not thrown from the Jeep that Reno had rolled began to crawl their way out of the wreckage. One of them threw his gun down while he inspected the magazine in his hand. He threw that away as well in frustration and began to march back up to the house with the others. The driver, a busty woman in a fur coat, passed around a flask for them each to take a drink just like the man in the house had done.

"Thirst. Is that it?" Simon snarled to himself. He huffed and morphed back to his wolf form to run toward where he had last seen Mama and Sam.

***

Tanya held onto Fisher's fur as they disappeared into the dark tunnel. She held on tight with her head low and hugged his body with her legs. The smell inside was terrible, like the city dump.

Fisher moved quickly and, when they came to a stop, he whined. She took it as a sign to dismount. Her feet settled on something uneven. She reached out to feel a wall made of wooden planks.

"This is it. I was just on the other side earlier tonight. A couple of hours ago, maybe." Her eyes adjusted slowly to the lights trying to peek between the boards blocking their way.

Fisher spoke back and made her jump. "That gas in here is making my head fuzzy. If I'm not mistaken, it's methane. And this door feels jammed."

Tanya reached out in the dark until she touched his shoulder. "If it's not too much to ask, do you think you can break through it?"

"I'll try. Stand back against the tunnel wall and be ready to move fast if it falls the wrong way." Fisher gave her a gentle push to be sure she was moving away.

He filled the space with his beastly form just long enough to slam the plank wall and get through. Tanya had to squint to handle the difference in brightness but moved through after him as he shrank back to his human frame.

"Hey, um… I was wondering how long you guys knew I was here?" Tanya asked nervously, trying not to sound selfish. "If you can just tear through walls, what stopped you from coming in after me?"

Fisher looked around at the open room and the bottle racks. "This is a lot of hooch. Someone must be pretty thirsty-" He spun around to look at her like he had forgotten she was there. "Oh! Well, if you want it straight… we weren't here for you. No offense. It's a long story, but somehow, Reno got caught, which, as you can imagine, is no small feat. And we had to wait for the right time to come in after him. Sam, too. And anyone who can capture two of us, well, that put us on edge about busting in half-cocked. And-" He trailed off as he looked closer at the bottles and muttered something about smuggling through the tunnel.

Tanya pulled his arm when he turned to face the racks again. "And what? Aren't you guys kind of always half-cocked?"

"No. Well, I mean, yeah, I guess so," he admitted. "But we needed to be sure you weren't part of the party in case we, you know, went off and got you hurt, too. In case Simon hasn't told you, we're not always totally in control. And when we lose control- Well, let's just say you don't look like a friend when things get to that point. You know what I mean?"

Tanya made an angry face and had to calm herself when she felt the heat in her cheeks. "I guess that means you got my message."

"Oh, I have no idea," Fisher confessed. "But if I didn't know before, seeing you chained up as bait for Reno cleared up which side you were on quickly. Sorry, I can't break those by the way. Bit too risky. There are a lot of little bones in your hand and wrist." He addressed the wine rack again, and began counting the totes and estimating the number of bottles. "Hey, so I have this theory about what's going on here. But... sorry, I'm sure you don't want to get into that right now. We really should get who you came for and get the hell out."

Tanya stopped him before he could start climbing the stairs that would lead him into the study with the pull-away bookcase. "I told you, it's my sister. Aren't you worried about all the crashing and shooting going on? Do you have any idea how many people are up there?"

Fisher stopped and shrugged. "I don't really know, but I don't think it'll matter much. With Sam and Reno out, the only reason I'm still here instead of trying to lead them away is because you won't leave, and I can't let you go in alone."

"Are you serious right now?" Tanya took hold of him by his jacket sleeve. "The odds are stacked against you, even with the pack. It would be suicide!"

He glared back, trying to intimidate her. "If you knew that, you wouldn't come back either, though. I tried to tell you-"

"No, stop! You don't understand. I meant to sneak back in."

"I'm not as good at that when indoors and outnumbered," Fisher admitted. "In this case, the best move is to plow directly through them. And you can find the key from whichever body you think is carrying it."

When he turned again to go up the steps, Tanya held on but followed along. "That's barbaric. Is it really the only way? I thought you said busting in was a terrible idea?"

"Oh, it's still a bad idea. But it's the most efficient and I won't have to be so careful. The problem is always the same, though. Once I turn, there's this... how do I describe it? The thing we can become has a chance to take over. And after that, we're just along for the ride. And it doesn't always wait for us to decide to bring it out either. If it becomes provoked or ignored for too long, it needs out and can force its way. Then, whatever happens, happens. I'm just banking on the idea that if all the shooting has gone on this long, that whatever secret weapon they had to capture us must not be an option anymore."

"Fisher, what the hell do you expect me to do? Wait down here until the screaming and crashing around stops and hope you haven't lost control and are waiting for me?" Tanya's mouth hung open like another alternative clung to her tongue but couldn't form words.

"That would be the best thing you can do," he said matter-of-factly. Fisher pushed at the bookcase when they reached it and peeked through the smallest opening he could manage. "But if you need something to pass the time, you can start smashing those bottles down there. Because if you don't, my theory is that the fight up here could go on for a long while. There's something about that stuff that's not right. And it may be part of a spiritual connection that protects this place. I haven't had time to sort out the details. though." He pulled her closer to the space so she could see. "I think we have a new problem, though."

Tanya heard Solomon's guests shouting back and forth at each other but couldn't see them in what little exposure they had to the main hall. But she saw the flickering of blue and red lights against the plain wall color contrasting the white chandelier lights.

"Did you guys call the police?" She looked back at him for answers, but Fisher shook his head with a shrug.

***

"Home stretch, guys," came Mo's voice in Blake's earpiece. "Next lane up on the right. I got eyes on the inside, finally. Some kind of party going on. Hold up, B, these guys are strapped up. Almost everyone in there has a gun."

Blake checked his mirror so the camera could see. "This is not a good time to stop. How many guns are we talking about?"

Mo's voice crackled against the poor signal, and the sirens chasing them didn't help. Blake looked over at Deacon riding beside him, but he only shook his head and tapped his helmet.

They made the final turn to see the only lights from the house were a second-floor spotlight pointing off into the dark and the downstairs windows had a glow shining out.

When Blake and Deacon had cleared the treeline, Mo's voice came in shouting, "Are you still on the line? I said they're armed to the teeth! There's too many to count. At least twenty."

Deacon looked over to Blake who revved his bike louder. "We got it, Mo. Thanks. Keep an eye out, but keep quiet a couple of minutes unless I need to hear something, okay?" Blake rechecked his mirror to see the police cars were slowing to take the turn. "Now, Deac! You go left, ditch the bike, and take cover."

Blake drove up where the driveway split and then circled in front of the double doors. He took the right side and laid

228

down his bike so it would slide down the bank and leave him close enough to some hedges to keep cover.

"Hey, Deac?"

"Yeah?"

"You still a good shot?"

"I do alright." Deac sounded confused. "You got a target in mind?"

"Shoot anything but the cops," Blake answered. "We're gonna need their firepower. But to get it, we'll have to draw it. Got me?"

Instead of answering, when the police cars came to a stop, a few shots rang out and hit a windshield and a headlight. Blake waited until he saw the doors open on the first stopped car and shot at the light bar and a side mirror.

"That one was for you, brother."

Deacon laughed but the voice of Agent Waites cut him off. "Gentry, what do you think you're doing? I just wanted you to take a look!"

"Long time, no talk. Hey, so there's more to the story here than your partner. Some asshole started shooting at your boys in blue, so now if you want me to get a better look, I need to get in behind whoever it is and find out what's going on."

Repeating rifle rounds shot from the house. Blake backed himself up against the nearest wall under a window as pistol shots returned fire, which he assumed were police shooting back.

Waites and Mo exchanged words during the gunfire that were hard to catch. "Automatic rifles? I'm calling in more backup."

"Lady, you could call in the Delta Force, but they ain't gonna get here in time!" Deacon laughed again. "I'm moving to the-holy shit!"

The glass shattered and more shots rang out. The window above Blake's head broke out as bullets whizzed by. When he braved a look into the house, bodies were flying across the large room. A beast took wide swipes with its claws at the party of shooters and moved almost too fast to follow.

"Attaboy, Simon."

A hand on his shoulder caught him off guard. "In over your head again?"

Blake flipped up his visor and turned to face Simon and grinned. "Just looking for a bathroom. If you're out here, then who is that?"

"Same old party crasher from our last Thanksgiving together." Simon grabbed Blake's collar. "I haven't seen this jacket in a while. I thought you gave up gang life?"

"Oh, you know how it goes. Some things are never over."

Gunfire continued and Simon spun to look in. "I better get in there. If you're smart, you'll stay outside."

Blake looked over Simon's shoulder and took a few shots at a man in a tuxedo with blood running down his face who was holding a rifle. Simon jumped and transformed before tackling the man who dropped his gun.

"Yeah, well, since when am I the smart guy?" Blake jumped in through the broken window and removed his helmet to see better. He crawled his way to a piece of art that had been knocked off the wall and adjusted his earpiece. As screams and shooting overwhelmed the large hall, he placed his helmet on a table to face the action.

"I hope you can still hear me," Blake said, holding his uncovered ear. "As long as that camera holds out, you'll be able to see better than if it's on my head."

Just as he crawled back to where he could barely see, two more of the werewolf pack crashed into the main hall, rattling the chandelier above and bringing down a shower of dust around it. He had to slink back out of the way as a man with a blond ponytail was flung against the wall beside him. Blake pushed his pistol up under the man's chin, pulled the trigger and then took his rifle.

A terrible roar echoed in the room. One of the werewolves had thrown the last man standing into the banister and the impact bent the body over backward with a sickening snap before it slumped to the stairs.

Chapter Twenty-Five - Once More, with Feeling

Tanya broke away from the bookcase door and ran into the main hall to start searching for Mr. Christian and the key. After a look around while the pack were collecting themselves, she could see him sprawled face-down at the bottom of the stairs and rooted into his pockets.

"He doesn't have it!" She pushed her hair back out of her face in frustration.

Deacon approached her and offered a hand up. "What are you looking for? We need to get you out of here before those cops start taking shots at you."

"You?! What the hell are you doing here?" Tanya spread her hands out in frustration and urgency. "I need the key. A skeleton key that fits the upstairs door. My sister is locked in that room!" She pointed up the stairs to the corner door.

Simon ran over to her and took her arm. "We can't stay here. There's no time-" Simon stopped at the sound of laughter in the middle of the room.

Tanya turned to Simon and started shaking as she saw his wounds. "Simon! I'm so close! I just need to get through that door!"

Reno was seething next to Solomon who was climbing to his feet with his tuxedo splattered with blood. Reno took a swing at Solomon that sent him back to one knee and he laughed again. He spat onto the floor and rose to his feet to throw a punch of his own. Reno's face turned with the blow and he retaliated by grabbing Solomon's belt and hair to hold him.

"What do you want to do with this piece of shit?" Reno asked Simon.

But when Simon turned away from Tanya, they both could see a police officer had breached the doors and had his gun pointed at them.

"Nobody moves! Everyone put their hands up where I can see them and get on your knees!" His face showed a cut across his cheek and a furious expression.

Tanya put her hands up and stayed near the stairs. The others slowly complied except for Reno.

Reno refused to release Solomon and dragged the man to the center of the room. "This scum is who you want. And I want justice for his crime against me." His chest and shoulders rose and fell like he was struggling to catch his breath.

Solomon spoke evenly to the policeman, "These people are trespassing on my property and saw fit to make a bloodbath of me and my friends. Sir, I need medical attention."

"I said I want to see your hands! Drop him and surrender yourself. We can talk downtown."

Another voice echoed out from the library door. "Officer,

I'm Agent Sterling with the ATF." Sterling showed his badge and wiped blood from a deep cut behind his ear. "I want all of them in cuffs before we proceed! Do you have adequate backup?" He walked around the bodies, in front of Tanya, then toward Reno under the chandelier.

Tanya noticed with the blood wiped away that the gash closed and healed seamlessly. She turned her head slowly to look down at Mr. Christian whose hand was creeping to push himself up.

She screamed out to draw the attention of everyone in the room. But by the time they turned, Mr. Christian held her in front of himself as a body shield and began walking her backward up the stairs. He held a rifle out from his waist with one hand and had a knife at her throat with the other. She released the chain that still clung to the handcuffs on her wrist and let it drag as she reached up at his strong arm. Her nails dug in and drew blood, but he held on tighter.

"Drop your weapon," Mr. Christian boomed. "Call your people off or the girl and both of you are going to pay for it." When they didn't immediately respond, Mr. Christian squeezed the trigger to shoot toward the floor. "I said drop it!"

When the officer laid his weapon down, he radioed from the device on his shoulder, "Officers will stand down and await further orders. This is now a hostage situation." Sweat beaded on his angry face.

Tanya again surveyed the room as she stepped up in reverse.

TAINTED WITH BLOOD

She saw the slowly crawling party guests moving closer to the officer and Agent Sterling. Her eyes widened in fear but Mr. Christian's arm pressed hard into her throat.

The cultists' bodies had been creeping closer and stood at once to overpower the police officer with a hand over his mouth as they beat him from every direction. Many of the others recovered with guns held out threatening the pack and the bikers. Tanya watched as they dragged Agent Sterling in front of Solomon and demanded Reno to let go of him.

Reno released his grip and Solomon turned to give a nod to Mr. Christian before bringing a knee up into Reno's gut. He stepped behind him and kicked down hard on the back of his knee to bring him down.

Mr. Christian turned Tanya toward the door where she had last seen Melissa and she could see the key already placed in the lock. "You made your way back into the house, so I'll reward you by letting you say goodbye to your sister. And then I'm going to watch her drain you for your efforts."

Tanya cried as he turned the key and opened the door. Melissa lay as she was before, splayed out on the bloodstained bedding. He pushed her into the room and the chain dragged with an unpleasant scrape across the hardwood.

The stake lodged in Melissa's chest was the same kind of tent spike attached to Tanya's chain.

She could hear Missy's voice in her head and cried at the sound as she approached the bed.

"Tilly! So close. Come closer." It was barely a whisper this time. It sounded to her as if Melissa was dying right in front of her.

"I can't, I can't!" Tanya cried. She reached with a shaking hand toward the spike. But before she could reach it, shots were fired and shattering glass sounded outside the room that drew Mr. Christian's attention. Tanya grabbed the spike and pulled before throwing herself to the floor and rolling under the bed.

***

Blake watched as the swarming guests circled Reno. A group of them left the room in a hurry and returned with several weapons Blake didn't expect to see, including a whip, a bat, a studded glove, and a variety of swords. They were distributed and each took a turn beating the werewolf for their host to watch. A woman in a fur coat kicked him in the gut with her high-heeled shoe. The heel broke and she took off both shoes to fling them across the room. A short, stout man punched him in the face, forcing him to spit blood on the man's shoes.

The man with the slick pompadour must have been the host. He began pacing patiently around with the whip wrapped around his shoulder as he rolled up his sleeves.

Mo spoke through the earpiece again, "B, I hope you see what I see. More than half of them gave up their guns. And unless they're clipped up, they should be all but empty after that shootout."

Blake surveyed the room to see how many guns were still drawn on the pack and Deacon after the circle had been armed with their new weapons. He looked to Simon, whose face was stone blank but with wide eyes. Simon shook his head 'no' when they locked eyes. He looked to Deacon, who had his hands clasped behind his head, and slowly lowered his chin. Deacon returned a careful nod.

Blake threw an elbow into the belly of the chuckling gunman next to him and shots were fired up toward the ceiling. Blake grabbed the gun hand and kept the rifle pointing at the chandelier as he stood up behind the man.

Blake took hold of the man's head and twisted with every ounce of strength he had, then held the body as a shield. He emptied the rifle with high shots in a spray across the circle. Bullets were flying all around the room again, as well as more from the police barricade outside.

A whip cracked and wrapped around the rifle, which pulled Blake to face the host. He dropped to his side on the floor and drew his shotgun from under his arm to fire. The blast knocked the host off his feet and Blake turned to fire another shot into the crowd coming at him.

One of the werewolves tackled the mob to one side and Blake could see Reno take two shots to the chest coming from the front doors. Blake ran toward the stairs and took Agent Sterling by the collar to cover around one side. He kicked in a door there behind the stairs.

"Well, tell Waites I found that bathroom," he joked. Blake pushed Sterling against a wall inside the door and pointed at his earpiece. "Your partner sent me to check up on you. So stay put. I don't know how you or anyone else made it this far."

"What? You can't expect-"

"I don't expect anything," Blake interrupted. "I did what I was told, and now I'm busy, capiche?"

"Wait, dammit! It's the drink! They swore me into their cult and made me drink this stuff in the cellar!" Sterling opened his bloody jacket and revealed a starched white shirt that was full of holes and even bloodier. His chest skin and hair were stained red but showed no signs of harm. "It has to be. And they've got plenty of it. It just has to be. I'm not some superhero."

Blake spoke to the microphone, "You catch all that, Deac? You need to find the cellar and have yourself a drink. Then destroy the rest. I'm working on a way out."

"I hear ya, bro. Surprised you managed not to get shot… aw, hijueputa!"

A hail of bullets rang out just outside the bathroom door. Blake looked out to see DX shooting at the ceiling until the chandelier fell and dropped. It burst into flames on the back of a werewolf fighting off a mob. The beast loosed a sickening howl and flailed its arms wildly in the fire, tossing flaming bodies in every direction. Blake ran out from cover and grabbed Deacon by his collar to guide him back while shooting over his shoulder.

Deacon's helmet was sideways, covering his eyes. "My helmet took a hit on one side. That was close." He unscrewed it until it came free and then discarded it with the earpiece.

Blake turned out the light and stood in the doorway, peeking out. A hail of bullets ripped into the wall and his left shoulder and he tucked into the bathroom. He pulled his pistol and fired blindly out the door. "Well, so much for not getting shot! I'm gonna try to get this guy out through a window. The one next to the chandelier is the closest. No offense, Sterling, but now I know you can take a shot, so you're my cover." He looked to Deacon and slapped his shoulder. "That cellar can't be hard to find. You'll make a run the other way and I'll find you when I can."

Deacon nodded and checked his clip. "I think I got about half a clip left, are you good?"

"Three left in the shotgun if my count is right," Blake groaned. "But I could pump these into our friend here and they wouldn't make any difference, would they?"

"I meant your arm, man. You'd have a better chance against one of your beast buddies out there with only three shots," Deacon joked as he looked at Blake's arm. He pulled his knife and cut a strip off of a hand towel to tie above Blake's elbow. "Hey, they are on our side, aren't they?"

"I'd mention you haven't been eaten yet, but that kind of talk is what got my shoulder shredded."

***

Melissa licked her lips and let Solomon's large bodyguard drop to the floor. She spotted a chain that led under the bed and pulled it until Tanya was dragged out into view. There was an awkward silence while the woman looked up from the floor in fear. Melissa took a step over her and slowly offered a hand. "Come on, Tilly, I've had about enough of this place."

Her sister stood on shaky legs and wrapped her arms around Melissa for the first time in over six years. She cried into her shoulder.

Melissa pushed her back gently. "Take his weapons if you need them. I imagine his benefactor is still breathing. I'll have to see to that."

"Missy, no!" Tanya pleaded. "Let's just go! They have some kind of protection."

Melissa placed a cold hand on Tanya's cheek. "And now, so do you. Do you know how to hurt them?"

Tanya hesitated, looking at the man on the floor, but then nodded. "I think so."

"Then show me the way."

Tanya grabbed the rifle and knife and started to wrap the chain again so it wouldn't drag. When they left the room, the main hall downstairs was only lit by a fire in the center of the floor and the flashing strobe of blue and red lights from outside.

Melissa dragged a finger along the railing as she surveyed the chaos below. "My kind of party. Remind me to thank our host for the invite."

Melissa leaped from the balcony and darted in a blur across the room. She plucked one of the curved swords from the floor and held it out to one side neck-high as she sprinted again at blinding speed in front of the human targets around the room, out of reach of the fiery, broken chandelier. She narrowly missed a lunge from a werewolf whose fur was ablaze as it jumped out the window to roll in the snow. When she crossed the open threshold, Melissa could see several police cars outside and officers taking cover between shots into the building. She could hear a helicopter out of sight but saw its spotlight shining through the door coming from the air. She kicked off the doorway to return to the stairs with another blade swipe across the room. She slid to a halt and threw away the saber to grab Tanya who had only just reached the bottom of the stairs.

"Come on, slowpoke," Melissa urged her sister. "Where are we going?"

Tanya led them toward the cellar and down the stone steps led by the bright string of lights. At the bottom, the room opened to show a large bottle rack and broken wooden planks at the foot of a large, dark opening.

Footsteps were coming down toward them and Melissa tucked Tanya behind herself. She held her ground as a brown-skinned biker with a braided ponytail entered the room at a run.

241

Deacon leaned against the wall to catch his breath. "Good to see you, blondie. I know it's not the time, but you kinda stood me up, ya know?"

Tanya peeked around Melissa. "I got caught up in a mess, I can explain later if we make it out alive. We have to destroy all this liquor or those freaks are going to keep getting up."

"I see you still keep only the best of company." Melissa scowled at the biker as he moved closer. "Are you here to stop us?"

"Stop you? No, I'm here to finish this." Deacon took a bottle off the shelf and broke the neck on the shelf to smell it. He took a long drink, spilling it down his chin and smashed the bottle on the floor. "Well, at least I won't feel bad about wasting it. This stuff is terrible! Breaking them all will take too long. But I have an idea. Do you know if that tunnel leads out?" He pulled a crushed pack of cigarettes from his jacket pocket and lit a curled and broken one. He grabbed two more bottles and broke them on the floor.

"I came in that way, it should be clear. Do you think this will work?" Tanya pointed toward the smashed tunnel door.

"If it doesn't, I guess we're all pretty fucked, aren't we?" Deacon threw the next bottle toward the place he pulled it from and splashed booze all over the old wooden rack. He pulled his sweater sleeve out from his wrist and used his knife to cut away the cuff. Deacon broke another bottle top and stuffed the small cloth into what was left of the neck, cutting his knuckles as he did. He waved away the pain, sucked a cut on his finger, and spat before he pulled his lighter again. "Get going, I'll be right behind you."

Melissa eyed his hands working and curled her lips with her tongue licking the inside. She stepped closer to the man and fought the urge to feed. She closed her eyes until Tanya's voice drew them.

"No, wait! That tunnel is full of gas!" Tanya held her hands up.

Deacon hurried over to the opening to smell. "Dios mio, it smells like a dump! Why the hell is there gas?"

Melissa took Tanya's hand. "He said we should go. So we should go." She pulled Tanya along to start up the stairs.

Deacon called after them, "Not that way, are you crazy?"

"I don't share your love for pyrotechnics," Melissa called back to him. "Good luck with that tunnel of death. I hope you can run fast."

Chapter Twenty-Six - What Doesn't Kill You

Simon shook off the blurry vision as he was forced back to his human form. Fisher stood over him, smacking his face.

"Hey, there you are. Had me worried for a sec." Fisher helped Simon to his feet. "They won't stay down. You're exhausted. This isn't our fight anymore." Fisher rolled his neck. "I'm going back in for Sam, but I need you to get Mama."

Simon crouched in the doorway to a darkened library with bare, dusty shelves. A spotlight outside shone through a window on the opposite side of the vast, mostly empty room as it flew by with the whipping sound of helicopter rotor blades.

"I think you're right. We can't keep doing this. I'm barely holding it together," Simon admitted. "I don't want us all going off the rails, that's what started this mess. What about Reno?" Simon asked as he watched the bodies begin to rise again.

"He was under the chandelier and burned. Then he split. I figure that's just the break we need to move. We'll find him out in the sticks if we can get clear of this damned place. Let's go!" Fisher gave a nod to Simon and ran back into the flickering hall.

Simon huffed and rubbed his hands together. His head pounded and he held his ribs. Where he lay a moment before, a handful of spent bullets remained and he noted fresh blood on his belly where they likely came from.

He approached the door and scanned the room to find Mama behind the staircase holding her head. He pushed his aching muscles to keep going and ran to meet her. Much of her backside was covered in blood and a gash across her throat was slowly closing. He scooped her up in his arms to run for a way out but, when he turned, the rising mob had surrounded them. He noticed some had grotesque burns and missing hair. The one woman among them was removing what was left of her tattered and singed fur coat and marching forward barefoot on a twisted leg. One man assisted another in setting a broken arm and many of them had long smears of blood soaking their clothing from the throat down.

Mama held onto him weakly in his arms. "I can't. The lights, the fire. The room is spinning. I've bled too much. I got nothing left. It's coming, Simon. I can't stop it."

"Just hold on a minute for me. I got you." Simon back-stepped his way toward the broken chandelier.

The flames had gone out among the broken pieces of crystal but had already spread to one wall where, Simon presumed, from the crumbling frame around the window, Reno made his escape. The fire climbed the heavy drapes and pieces of upturned and broken furniture lining the walls between openings.

The mob closing in wore menacing grins. Some held rifles as if they were baseball bats. Some had knives or swords.

245

The man that Simon recognized with his pompadour stood behind the crowd, holding a bottle above his head with both hands. He turned the bottle over and emptied it onto himself, the liquid showering his face and tuxedo. The crowd of cultists began chanting a muddle of words that Simon couldn't comprehend at first. The chant became clear as he spun around looking for a gap to run through that might be the least threatening.

"Take with thee this night, guide thine eyes without sight.
Soak thine flesh from within, may thee unburden thy sin.
Test thy will by trial, forsaking beholden denial.
May blood-tainted spirits wake, thirst of thine soul to slake."

Simon growled to himself, "Drowning in spirit. Can't see the storm. Shifting current. Dammit Joshua, what does it mean?" He knelt with Mama and looked into her face. He rubbed his thumb under her mouth where blood clung to her lip. "Pray for us, Phie."

A rumble shook the house and dropped many of the mob to their knees and into each other. Another thundering roll of explosive sounds followed it and carried on for several seconds as the floor shook. The ceiling split as Simon followed with his eyes. Over the heads of the shambling cultists, Simon saw policemen at the doors and windows pointing their guns and shouting commands. He looked back down. Mama's eyes were barely open, showing the bright yellow color of her beast trying to come out just before the floor broke through under them. He held onto Mama with all his might and braced to take the fall. The crumbling debris struck the cellar floor causing a backdraft fireball from the flames below.

***

From the top of the stone steps, Tanya steadied Mr. Christian's rifle to shoot into the swarming cultists when the floor shook. She braced herself in the doorway and looked back down to see if Deacon chose to follow. A blast from below and a sudden fiery flash told her it was too late.

The house quaked again and she turned just in time to see the mob tumbling into each other enough to reveal Simon kneeling in the middle of them holding Mama. Solomon locked eyes with Tanya and laughed madly from the other side as he held a bottle upside-down over his head like a sacred artifact. When the floor fell under them, Tanya dropped the gun and ran into the crumbling room. Before she could reach the collapse to look, a ball of fire erupted out from the pit that knocked Tanya back off her feet.

Solomon, engulfed in flames, ran flailing and screaming toward her. Tanya handed the spike from her chain to Melissa and unwound the links from her arm. The sisters split apart and Melissa blurred around him, wrapping his neck and planting the spike in his chest. He reeled backward at the edge of the pit.

Melissa cocked her head to one side. "How does that feel, darlin'?"

"Missy! The chain!"

The slacked links on the chain pulled taut as Solomon fell. Melissa took Tanya's hand and crushed it with her powerful grip. Tanya screamed as the cuff slipped off her wrist. She buried her face in Melissa's neck and slunk to the floor cradling her crippled hand.

Holding his bloody arm, Blake emerged from behind the blazing grand staircase with David Sterling following close behind.

Tanya sat in the rubble and sobbed as flames from the fireball spread across the cracked ceiling.

Melissa crouched beside her, glaring over Tanya's shoulder. "I can fix this, but we need to go. Come with me."

Tanya tried to stand when she saw Agent Sterling in a blood-soaked shirt being led by Blake across the floor. A werewolf crashed through the ceiling in between Melissa and Blake. Two shotgun blasts rang out and she saw Blake push Sterling to the floor, revealing the biker's wounded shoulder. The beast wrapped its enormous paw, with one digit missing, around Blake's face and threw him to the floor before the sisters. Blood ran from his face into his hair and he lay motionless with his chest heaving.

The werewolf howled but, before he could attack, two others leaped up from the pit and tore into the injured one with its missing claw. They flanked it and traded blows until they overpowered it onto its back. Tanya didn't close her eyes in time before the two attackers tore out its throat and ripped the head away.

She turned and saw Melissa stooped over Blake's body, drinking from his neck. "Missy! Oh, my God, no!"

Melissa smoothed Blake's hair away from his bloodied face and crooked her head back to look at Tanya with doll-like black eyes. "We're out of time. If you stay, you might be able to save him. But if you come with me-"

"How could I just leave him?"

Melissa stood and lowered her eyes, then she mouthed a word as a flurry of bullets ripped through her torso. Tanya looked toward the shooter to see Deacon held a gun and shot through what was left of the hanging plastic. When his eyes went wide, she looked back at Melissa. A man she had never seen before held her sister in his arms.

His face was pale and waves of black hair fell over one eye as he bent to look at Melissa closely. "Come, Little Flower. You've been sorely missed."

With a swirl of dark mist, they were both gone.

Deacon slid across the floor and put his head against Blake's chest. "Stay with me, bro!"

Sterling ran to help pick up Blake and looked at Tanya. "Can you walk? This place is coming down!"

Tanya looked back once more as burning debris fell from the ceiling. The werewolves were gone except for the rent and decapitated body of Reno in a pool of blood on the floor near the stairs. She stood and chanced a look into the pit while clutching her broken hand. She saw a pile of burned bodies but could not identify Solomon's face among them. Her eyes scanned again and welled with angry tears. She spun around to watch the strobe of police lights competing with flames. She spun slowly in place, caught in a trance, like she was dancing to a song played by the overhead chopper blades until it all faded to black.

Chapter Twenty-Seven - Miles to Go Before I Sleep

Tanya woke up in a hospital bed. Her eyes drew to a splint on her wrist. She tried to move her fingers and wretched as her face twisted with pain.

There was an IV connected to the opposite hand, with the tube leading up to a small hanging bag of clear fluid that was nearly empty. Although every part of her body ached, she sat up and saw David Sterling folding a magazine closed as he stood next to her. Her mouth dropped open and her lip trembled upon seeing him. A blue vinyl curtain was pulled around most of the bed, blocking the door.

He shushed her gently like he might a child. "Easy now, I'm a friend. You've been through hell. And you look like it, too."

"I… I need to get up. I need to find, uh, Mr. Gentry."

"You're a friend of his? I can take you to him. You may want to get yourself dressed first, though. I had an officer go bring some things from your boutique that matched sizes with what you were wearing." Sterling took her uninjured hand. "Mr. Gentry is under special watch. I should tell you he lost a lot of blood. He suffered a terrible knock on the head. But they tell me he's showing good numbers."

Tanya looked at a marker board on the wall that read

Tanya Johnston
broken hand, scaphoid fracture
avulsion fracture (2), dislocated wrist.

"I'm Agent Sterling, by the way. I'm with the ATF." Sterling shook her hand gently to formalize their introduction. "I hope you're lucid enough to tell us what you were doing with Adam Solomon."

"I can't answer that right now. I need to see my friend first."

Sterling sighed and nodded with hesitation. "Alright, I'll tell you what. I'll take you down to see him. Maybe afterward we can talk?"

"Yeah, sure. Whatever. I just need to see him. I have to thank him."

She took his hand for help to stand and he excused himself to the other side of the curtain so she could dress.

Tanya wasted no time pulling the tape and IV out with her teeth so she could get into the change of clothes without the tube in the way. Even in her hurry to get out of this room, she couldn't help but scrunch her nose at the shimmery purple leggings and gray college sweater with plaid lettering. She slipped into flat, brown moccasins that were surprisingly comfortable and pulled back the curtain.

Sterling opened the door for her where she saw Mo sitting in a chair holding a lidded paper cup on his bouncing knee. Mo

252

stood upon seeing her but Agent Sterling stepped between them.

Mo's nostrils flared, his chest puffed, and he glared at the agent.

Sterling stepped aside and offered, "Alright kids, alright. I'll see if I can find a decent cup of coffee. I guess you know where you're going."

When Mo turned back from watching Sterling leave, Tanya leaned into him and cried with her arms around his neck. "How did you know?"

He spoke softly, "It doesn't matter right now. All that matters is you're okay."

"Oh, God, I can't believe you're here!" Tanya lifted her head and looked into his eyes. "I've been the worst. I'm so sorry. I should have stayed with you and-"

"And what? And never found out where Missy was?" Mo rolled his lip and held her chin up so she wouldn't look away. "I told you, I got you. We've got something real whether we're a thing or not. I'm not going anywhere."

Tanya leaned into his warm hand and kissed the palm. She looked down to see he was still holding a cup in his other hand. "Is that boba in that cup?"

"Maybe. What makes you think it's not something for me?" He tried to stay serious, but his eyes wrinkled at the corners, giving him away. "But I have to admit that I usually only buy drinks for girls that dress better than this. Someone with taste."

Tanya pouted, closed her eyes, and leaned her head back but then winced at the brightness of the fluorescent hospital hall light. "Would you make an exception if the girl right in front of you is seeing stars?" She squinted until her eyes adjusted.

Mo let out a playful sigh. "Just this once, but don't tell my sister. She has this habit of telling my business to this chick I really like."

A frizzle-haired brunette nurse in flowery scrubs stopped with a chart balanced against her hip to interrupt them. "Alright folks, let's keep the hall clear, this is an emergency room, not a park bench."

Mo stepped back and apologized, then guided Tanya along by her elbow, careful to keep her wrapped hand from bumping against him. "So, Blake's still under close watch at the far end of this ward. I got down there not long ago. They had to hit him with the paddles and put nodes on his chest to monitor. I think they were setting him up for a transfusion. You guys went through some shit, huh?"

Tanya nodded and wrapped her arm around his back to lean again as they walked. "I'd prefer to forget, but I doubt I ever will."

She overheard a redheaded woman near them ask a lean, handsome Indian doctor about the name Von Croy. The woman pointed with a nod and turned toward the hall to the elevators.

"Hey, I think that was-," Tanya started but was trying to pay attention.

Mo looked at her, bewildered. "Are we looking for someone else?"

Tanya pulled away and leaned to get another glimpse as the woman raised her glasses into her hair.

A team of EMTs and nurses rushed a gurney down the hallway toward them and Tanya and Mo had to sidle up near the nurses' station. The elderly patient had a respirator mask on with his bare chest exposed. Tanya pulled on Mo's sleeve to follow the redhead to the elevators. "Come on."

"But Blake is on this floor, just further down," Mo reminded her.

Tanya bared her teeth like she was trying to share a secret. "I know, but if that woman said what I think she said, that's Simon's last name. She might be his mother. And if she's going upstairs, she's here for someone other than Simon. If he was here, he'd still be in the ER, right? And if she was leaving, the exit is back the way she came from."

"Alright, I guess." Mo sounded confused. "What's your point?"
They turned to the elevators as one was closing and watched to see where it stopped, then followed up in the car next to

it. When they reached the second floor, a sign indicated they were in the intensive care unit.

It was quieter than the emergency room. Tanya pointed to the woman she was following at a flecked blue desk asking a squatty receptionist with a dirty blonde bun, "Why wasn't I notified?"

The receptionist apologized, "I'm sorry, ma'am, sometimes we get a lot of patients and need to move some beds around. Your husband is in room 227."

The redhead replied, "Alright, thank you. Which way is the nearest restroom?"

Tanya bumped Mo with her elbow and started toward ascending numbers until they reached 227.

A fit, tanned male nurse wagged his finger in front of them. "At this hour, immediate family only."

Tanya lied, "I was on my way to see my father but had a little accident in a snow drift. I was told he just got moved into 227."

"Your name, miss?"

"It's Gutierrez, we're newlyweds. Is it okay if my husband is up here with me?"

The nurse apologized. "Yeah, but you need to sign in, alright?"

Tanya turned to Mo, "Would you take care of that for me, honey? And if you see Mom, let her know I'm here."

Mo nodded along and returned to the desk with a twisted-lipped expression.

Tanya entered room 227 to see a man with a full head of white hair and tired, baggy blue eyes waving her in. "Sweetheart, could you please hand me my newspaper?"

She moved closer and retrieved a perfectly folded newspaper that showed a half-finished crossword puzzle to hand to the man. He looked for a moment with darting eyes and licked his thumb to flip to the front page.

"Oh, shoot! It's darn near February," he said. "My boy's birthday is just a few days away and here I am, stuck in this bed with the flu!" He coughed and let the paper rest on his belly. "I'm sure he'll be along here any minute. Good boy, my Simon. Handsome kid. So smart, too. He's got my eyes, and his mother's- Well… she's not with us anymore. I've got Joan now, picking up after us sloppy boys." He laughed and folded his hands as he continued, not giving her room to speak. "I hate to forget my manners but if you could give me some privacy before he gets here, I'd be very grateful to you, sweetheart. He'll be fifteen this year, darn near a man himself. And I'm afraid I'm wrestling with how to tell him some bad news. If you see my Simon, ask him to bring his old man another blanket, would you?"

Tanya couldn't speak. She nodded, forced a smile, and left the room fighting back tears. She gestured to Mo and returned with him to the elevator.

Mo gave her a moment to find words then asked, "Do you want to talk about it?"

"Maybe on the way home. Can I crash at your place til I'm okay to drive? I still want to try to see Blake before we go, though."

He nodded and kept his hands in his pockets to give her what little space he could. "Whatever you want."

When they turned to the hallway to find Blake, Agent Sterling was there sipping coffee with a slender woman in a peacoat.

"He's one tough bastard, that's for sure," Sterling remarked to Tanya. "I owe him one."

Tanya looked through the tiny square window of one of the swinging doors. He had one red tube and one clear tube in his arm at the elbow, and a respirator automatically dispensing oxygen at a steady pace. Above his head hung a heart monitor with waves of electronic blue and green readings.

They stood in silence as if they might disturb the masked nurse inside recording data from a mounted computer screen.

The four of them stepped back when they heard footsteps hurrying toward them. They looked up to see the same red-haired woman they'd followed with a hand over her mouth. She had a desperate look and wailed at the window.

Tanya noticed the woman's knees wobbling just before both Mo and Sterling lurched forward to catch her as she fell. She sobbed in their arms all the way to a chair in front of an aquarium. The woman in the peacoat offered a tissue and knelt in front of the crying woman.

"Can I get you something, ma'am? How do you know that man?" Agent Sterling asked.

The redhead nodded but didn't speak. Flooded with emotions, she closed her eyes tight and squeezed the agent's hand for comfort.

From behind them, Tanya heard another familiar voice. "Gilly, Tanya! ¡Dios mio! Where were you? Did he wake up?" Gia was out of breath and distressed.

Mo shook his head and pushed a finger to his lips when he gestured toward the redheaded woman. He whispered, "Are you staying with him?"

Gia gave him a look from the corner of her eye after a glance at the other people sitting near the fish tank. She threw her hands up and tried not to sound upset. "My shift starts in an hour." She wiped a thumb under her eyes. "Would you order some food delivered to me in a few hours? I've got a twelve today on no sleep. I'll update you every hour."

Mo hugged Gia and she kissed his cheek. "Call me if you need anything else."
Tanya turned to Mo again and told him it was time to go if he was ready. "Do you mind driving in this?"

"You could stay and get some observation and meds on

demand," Mo offered.

"I'm okay. I need to get away from this, though. These lights. And the cold floors, I'm so tired of the cold! I need a heavy blanket and someone to hold me til I fall asleep."

"Alright, then." Mo took her by the elbow again. "Let's get you discharged and clear to go home."

Epilogue - Not too Hot, Not too Cold

The sun set on the first day of spring with layers of chromatic allure. Stars twinkled around a mysterious new moon and the few clouds were thin and wispy, like careless brush strokes on a twilight canvas.

Tanya checked her blonde curls in the tiny mirror of Deacon's motorcycle as the street lights flickered on. She scoffed at the sudden glare in the reflection and finger-dabbed her lipstick evenly.

"Come on, Deac! I'll be late."

Mo's voice in her Bluetooth® earpiece made her stand up straight, "When are you gonna dress up nice for me, T?"

"When you get the balls to dance with me in public," Tanya retorted. "And I'm talking ballroom, live music, hors d'oeuvres, champagne. Something that deserves all this work. Wait, can you see me?"

"You're still across the street, so, yeah," Mo answered.

"Where's the cam?"

"I'll put it on when we get there, it's in the corsage. I don't want to crush it when I'm holding onto this big, handsome biker."

Mo faked a laugh. "Ah! Funny! He's not even there, I told you I could see."

Tanya turned to the street and picked a dark window nearby to flip her finger at. She shook her hand out when her wrist cracked. "Oof! Could have used another couple days in the splint."

"A week would've been better. You alright?"

"I'm fine. It's not like I'm on my way to-"

A box truck rolled by, too loud for her last few words to be heard, but she smiled at the dark window as if she'd just thrown a satisfying insult.

Deacon came up the cement steps from the nearby building. "Sorry to keep you waiting. Live shows don't care about the clock. I'm starting to get into this stuff." Deacon threw a leg over the seat and adjusted his mirror. "What did I say about touching my bike?"

Tanya pulled on a leather jacket and spun to see if the rhinestones caught the light. On the back, between the studs, read HARLEE RIGGS in white sequins.

"You're gonna wear your show duds?"

"Just for the ride. I packed the rest in your saddle bag. I'll change when we get there so I don't mess it up on the way." Tanya threw a fishnet leg and spiked high heel over to mount the seat, looked up at the window to wave, and scooted tight against Deacon with a grin.

Deacon fastened a soldier-style helmet into place and started the engine. "You sure you don't want a helmet?"

"You ever wreck a bike?"

"Yeah, but only when I'm being shot at or chased," he laughed.

Tanya squeezed her arms around him. "Ugh! Yeah, just get me there on time so I can fix my hair." She grabbed his helmet as he offered it. "As it is, I don't have a lot of time to primp and preen again when we get there."

When he stopped outside a gated estate, Deacon asked if he should escort her to the door. "I can walk you up, or hang around if you want?"

Tanya took off her jacket and nudged Deacon forward so she could fully open the saddle bag. "It's a private investor banquet. And besides, you're not dressed for it. I just need your mirror for one more second before you go."

She carefully unrolled a bundle of lacy material. She pulled from it and put on a pair of black, leafy patterned bell sleeves, and secured them above her biceps. Then she fanned out a cutaway skirt that matched and fastened it at her waist. In the mirror, she pinned on the red rose corsage and adjusted the petals so the camera could see. She rolled her jacket into the saddle bag and gave Deacon a quick peck on the cheek.

"Don't wait up, boys!"

The last touch to the outfit was a half mask, which was so small it was almost an eye patch, with a black feathery fan around the outside. She was delighted to see the feathers hadn't bent in the bundle. She pressed the call box and the gate opened.

A postured, white-haired gentleman wearing a skull-like mask with bony fingers spread across his mouth opened the door to greet her. He wore a classic, black, tailcoat tuxedo with a silvery pin at the collar instead of a traditional bowtie. He took her hand with a subtle bow but didn't speak. Tanya looked closely to see that a smile reached his elderly eyes.

She took his arm and he walked her into a grand ballroom. Once inside, two gentlemen in simple tuxes closed the heavy doors behind them, which seemed to bring out the sparkle of the pristine, beaded crystal chandelier. A large gathering of men and women in the middle of the floor showed their variety of masks in place. They surrounded a man in a gray, striped, knee-length jacket with a pearly silk ascot. He also wore a bright white phantom mask that covered half his face.

When Tanya was shown in, the crowd parted toward the bald, phantom-masked gentleman, and her elderly escort announced her. "Ladies and gentlemen, our guest of honor has arrived."

Mo chirped in her ear with static. "What's going on? There's only one dude there?"

Tanya heard a door click at the top of a massive curved staircase. A couple stood at the top railing to wave before they turned to descend the stairs. The man wore a dress overcoat with a string bow at his neck and a golden, armored knight mask that covered his entire face. The woman on his arm wore an elegant wine-red dress with a split side up to her hip and a mask of flower petals that matched her dress. Her familiar dark hair and the way she moved made Tanya's jaw drop.

The couple parted the crowd from the other side and handed a glass of champagne each to Tanya and the man in gray. She recognized Melissa's features this close with no question as she politely took the glass. The knight-masked man shook hands with the phantom-masked one who, she now saw, was none other than Adam Solomon. He no longer had his perfect pompadour of black hair but rather a scarred, bald head. Tanya turned her head to hide the unmasked portion as politely as she could as Solomon looked her over.

Solomon raised a glass to propose a toast with a quick, awkward look around when he noticed no other glasses were raised. "Mister Atticus Fletcher! I want to thank you for your warmth, your welcome, and your champagne," he laughed. "Won't you introduce me to these two ladies? I've not yet had the pleasure."

TAINTED WITH BLOOD

The voice of the host, Mr. Fletcher, had a sweet, heavy European accent. "I believe you already have, Mr. Solomon."

Melissa removed her mask and winked at Tanya. Melissa's voice in her mind came, "Show him, Tilly. He needs to see." She spoke aloud to Solomon, "Oh, my dear Mr. Solomon, are you still searching for things you can't break?"

"Yes. Won't you... enlighten us?" Tanya acted quickly and removed her mask. Her chest was heaving and her heart was beating so fast. Her mouth dried immediately and she had to steel her lip to keep it from quivering.

The circle around them closed as Solomon's joyous smile drained into pale despair.

The golden knight-masked man swept Melissa away toward the stairs and announced, "Our guest offered a toast, my friends. I believe the etiquette is to drink to his health!"

Tanya stepped backward as the guests closed in on Solomon. He disappeared from her sight as they surrounded him.

"T, what's happening?" Mo asked. "Why the hell is that guy dancing with himself? He looks like he's drowning!"

Tanya whispered, "I'll explain later. Cut the camera and the call, okay?"

When Tanya looked up for Melissa, she and the knight-masked man were ascending the stairs almost as if floating until they reached the railing at the top to look down over the swarm of guests. Tanya turned to hurry for the door and was greeted by the older man in the skull mask.

He stood in her way and bowed again. "Miss Johnston, leaving so soon? The party is not yet over."

About the Author

Brian's debut novel, Bought with Blood, released in October of 2023. With much excitement to continue the story, he submitted the final draft of the sequel, Tainted with Blood, in December of 2024, less than a month before his untimely departure from this world.

Always the showman, his storytelling style was primarily influenced by cinema and theater. He hoped readers would be as captivated by the suspense and intrigue of the sequel as they were by the original high-octane thriller.